One Yea

Four sisters, four seasons, four weddings!

When their father dies unexpectedly, the Waverly sisters are set to inherit the beloved outback family estate. The only problem? An arcane stipulation in the will that requires all four of them to be married within a year or they'll lose the farm for good! But with such little time, how on earth will they each find a husband? Well...

Matilda is secretly already married—to a *prince* no less! Now she just needs to track him down...

in *Secretly Married to a Prince* by Ally Blake

Eve spends a night of distraction with a tattooed stranger, and the consequences are binding!

in *Reluctant Bride's Baby Bombshell* by Rachael Stewart

Available now!

Ana turns to her best friend for help. But their marriage of convenience is quickly complicated by *in*convenient feelings...

in *Cinderella and the Tycoon Next Door* by Kandy Shepherd

And Rose makes a deal with the devil: the strip of land his family—and the Waverlys' longtime rivals— has been after for years in exchange for a temporary marriage!

Claiming His Billion-Dollar Bride by Michelle Douglas

Coming soon!

Dear Reader,

When I was invited to this project by the fabulous Aussie trio Ally, Kandy and Michelle, several thoughts went through my mind. I'm not good enough. I don't want to let them down. I'm not Australian—lol!

Once I'd talked myself down from the panic, I realized I was being ridiculous and intimidated by my own fangirling. You see, I love these ladies. Their books bring me such joy and the idea that I could spin a tale worthy of their own was a big deal.

I'm so glad I said yes. Working with them, bouncing ideas around, sharing snippets and generally getting giddy with our stories has been a thrill. I hope you feel that excitement, camaraderie and love between these pages. They became sisters to me, just as our sisters came to being within the stories.

As for the tale, the outback makes for a cracking setting, and seeing Eve, my estranged sister, become comfortable in her own skin and return to the place where she belongs, learning to trust love, was a joy. And Nate—the tattooed lawyer with a heart of gold— he's my kind of hero in every way... Hope you agree!

Rachael x

Reluctant Bride's Baby Bombshell

Rachael Stewart

Recycling programs
for this product may
not exist in your area.

ISBN-13: 978-1-335-59667-3

Reluctant Bride's Baby Bombshell

Copyright © 2024 by Rachael Stewart

For questions and comments about the quality of this book, please contact us at CustomerService@Harlequin.com.

TM and ® are trademarks of Harlequin Enterprises ULC.

Harlequin Enterprises ULC
22 Adelaide St. West, 41st Floor
Toronto, Ontario M5H 4E3, Canada
www.Harlequin.com

Printed in U.S.A.

Rachael Stewart adores conjuring up stories, from heartwarmingly romantic to wildly erotic. She's been writing since she could put pen to paper—as the stacks of scrawled-on pages in her loft will attest to. A Welsh lass at heart, she now lives in Yorkshire, with her very own hero and three awesome kids—and if she's not tapping out a story, she's wrapped up in one or enjoying the great outdoors. Reach her on Facebook, Twitter (@rach_b52) or at rachaelstewartauthor.com.

Books by Rachael Stewart

Harlequin Romance

Billionaires for the Rose Sisters
Billionaire's Island Temptation
Consequence of Their Forbidden Night

Claiming the Ferrington Empire
Secrets Behind the Billionaire's Return
The Billionaire Behind the Headlines

How to Win a Monroe
Off-Limits Fling with the Heiress
My Unexpected Christmas Wedding

Surprise Reunion with His Cinderella
Beauty and the Reclusive Millionaire
My Year with the Billionaire

Visit the Author Profile page
at Harlequin.com.

For my writer sisters,
Ally, Kandy and Michelle,
Love you ladies!
xxx

Praise for
Rachael Stewart

"This is a delightful, moving, contemporary romance.... I should warn you that this is the sort of book that once you start you want to keep turning the pages until you've read it. It is an enthralling story to escape into and one that I thoroughly enjoyed reading. I have no hesitation in highly recommending it."

—*Goodreads* on *Tempted by the Tycoon's Proposal*

PROLOGUE

London,
June

EVE STARED AT her laptop screen. The video-call countdown glared back at her, mocking her every attempt to remain composed.

She checked her bun. Not a blonde wisp out of place.

Smoothed down her royal-blue power suit. Not a crease.

Scanned her office backdrop. Not a thing out of place. The glass and monochrome oozed success and sophistication. Everything she wanted to portray.

You've got this, she mentally coached.

Only she hadn't and no amount of talking herself up would change that.

Her father had been dead a month. A *month*. And she hadn't shed a tear.

She hadn't attended his state funeral back in Australia. She hadn't stood by her sisters as they and the nation mourned him. She hadn't let herself think about him at all.

But now she had to.

She was being forced to dial in for the reading of his will.

A will she couldn't care two hoots about. She wanted nothing of his. Nothing to remind her of the life she'd left behind in Australia a decade ago. She had everything she needed here in London. A great life, a great apartment, and a great job as a PR exec with a reputation that people twice her age would covet.

Which is why you've got this!

She'd spent her entire adult life perfecting her appearance as well as that of others. This was just another chance to shine.

For appearances were everything.

They could hide a multitude of sins and take you far too.

The former she'd got from her parents. The latter from her grandparents, who'd taken her in when she'd discovered said sins and fled Australia for the UK.

It was her grandparents who'd taught her how to play society's game—how to talk, how to walk, how to command the room. How to lose the gangly awkwardness she'd grown up with, too. An awkwardness that had seen her own father nickname her Bambi. Bambi!

Was it any wonder Eve had spent her early teens permanently hunched over, trying to blend into the background while hoping one day she'd be as lucky as Cinders and Prince Charming would come along and sweep her off her feet.

Just as her father had her mother.

That was until Eve's eyes had been opened to the truth—their love, a *lie*—and she'd quit daydreaming. Thrown her romance books aside for business and finance. Success she could trust. Love not so much.

And success was hers. Listed in *Management Today*'s prestigious 'thirty-five under thirty-five' of the UK's highest-achieving young businesswomen at only twenty-eight, she'd truly made it.

And, in so doing, become someone her father would have been proud of…if she'd ever given him the chance to know her again.

Too late, now.

And too late to prepare.

The screen came alive, presenting a room so achingly familiar she feared she'd crack a tooth.

Dark wood, panelled walls, leather furnishings that she could feel beneath her fingertips if she were to put her mind to it…she balled her hands on the desk before her.

Dad's office at the heart of Garrison Downs. She should have known that was where they would be.

As one of Australia's largest cattle stations set deep in the Outback, it was famed throughout the country for its one and a half million hectares, tens of thousands of cattle, red dust and craggy vistas, ghostly gum trees and its own precious river. The room she was looking at now having featured in magazines and TV broadcasts, played host to world leaders and stars from agriculture, industry, and movies alike.

But when she was growing up, it had been Dad's office. Just Dad. Eve hadn't cared about the fame or the fortune. Only that he was her father and the station had been her home.

And what a messed-up joke that was.

She tightened her fists, forced herself to focus on the present rather than the past. The camera was set back, gifting her a decent view of the people in the room. Most were suited and booted, some were huddled in groups, others hovering aloof. More than she would have expected and only three that she recognised.

Dad's lawyer, George Harrington, sat behind her father's desk, his ageing form swamped by the solid dark wood.

Closest to her and easily identifiable by her blonde waves sat Matilda. Though sat didn't quite cover the curled-up, broken form her little sister represented on the velvet sofa and Eve's heart winced. Her lashes flickering as she fought the urge to reach out, wondering why Rose, their big sister, wasn't doing just that.

But Rose was sitting in the guest chair before their father's desk, stiff-backed and still. *Too* still.

Cut from the same cloth as their father but with the softness of their late mother, Rose had always been a beacon of strength. A tower of support. Only as Eve looked at her now, brown hair scraped back in a no-nonsense ponytail, workwear on, she'd clearly come straight from the land, no second spared. Still pushing on and giving Garrison Downs her all when life had thrown its biggest curve ball yet—the sudden death of a man she'd idolised because Rose, like most others, didn't know any better...

Was it possible that beneath her own front her big sister was crumbling, too?

'Ah, Evelyn!'

She stiffened as Harrington spoke, drawing the attention of the entire room her way.

'Can you hear me okay?'

She had the ridiculous urge to duck. A response that in no way reflected the woman she was now and, angry with herself for daring to think it, she straightened. 'I can hear you perfectly fine, Mr Harrington.'

Rose's shoulders twitched and Matilda started to turn.

'Please proceed.' Eve spoke before her sister could. She didn't want Matilda to address her, she didn't want *any* sisterly talk. Not in front of a room full of people she didn't know, and not when she was feeling at her most vulnerable.

A sense she hadn't experienced in too long and had no idea how to handle.

'Very well...' Harrington cleared his throat '...we'll get straight to business.'

And so it began, the reading of the will, an outline of their father's wealth and its distribution...

words, just words, and Eve was numb to it all. The figures, the properties, the stocks and the shares. None of it a surprise. All of it vast. She might not respect Holt as a father or as a husband, but she couldn't fault his savvy handling of all things financial.

And then Harrington shifted gears, from the business to the personal, and Matilda shifted in her seat, her pain increasingly evident.

Move, Rose, she silently urged.

But it wasn't Rose who obeyed. It was River. Their father's old lilac border collie. He appeared in the lower half of the screen and joined Tilly on the sofa. Eve eased back, grateful to the dog for giving her sister the comfort she so dearly wished to give but hadn't been able to face a homecoming for…

Coward.

Harrington gave a rumbling cough, drawing Eve out of her self-reproach.

'To my daughters,' he was saying, 'I leave all of the above, and all my worldly possessions not listed hereupon, including, but not limited to, the entirety of Garrison Downs.'

As expected. As it should be.

And Eve would swiftly hand over her share to her sisters at the earliest opportunity.

'Let it be known,' Harrington went on, 'that it is my wish that my eldest daughter, Rose Lavigne Waverly, take over full control of management of Garrison Downs. If that is her wish. If not, I bow to her choice.'

Again, just as it should be. So why did Rose flinch?

Did her sister not anticipate this? Who else could possibly take it on? No one knew the land and the job as she did…

'At this point,' Harrington said, eyes sweeping over the guests, 'could we please clear the room of everyone bar family?'

Slowly, the room emptied out, every delayed second playing on Eve's nerves. When, finally, it was just them, Harrington gave a warm, sympathetic smile. 'Now that was quite the ask, I know. But necessary to cover all the intricacies of your father's will, with those who will best help you manage the ongoing running and reputation of the station…'

Eve couldn't care, she only wished she'd been gifted the chance to leave with the others.

'…there is just one more thing.'

He paused to rub a hand across his brow and Eve got the distinct impression he was delaying… but why?

Something was up. Something big. And bad.

Eve braced herself, ears straining.

'There is a condition placed over the bequest. One that has been attached to the property since its transfer to your family years ago.'

The lawyer removed his glasses and laid them on top of the papers in front of him.

'As I'm sure you know, the history of Garrison Downs is complicated, what with your great-great grandmother having won the land from the Garrison family in a poker match in 1904.'

Complicated? More like stupid.

To Eve's mind, if the Garrisons had been willing to risk their lands in a game, they deserved to lose them. And it wasn't as if they'd suffered too greatly. They still owned and ran Kalku Hills, a huge station in the south.

But the locals loved to big it up. The legend that was the poker match, the rivalry between the two families, the hatred...

'Any time the land has been passed down since,' Harrington continued, 'certain conditions had to be met.'

Conditions? Eve's gaze narrowed as the lawyer donned his glasses once more, hands unsteady as he lifted the papers to read directly from them.

'Any male Waverly heir, currently living, naturally inherits the estate,' he said, giving Rose a fleeting look when she murmured something Eve couldn't catch. 'But if the situation arises where there is no direct male heir, any and all daughters, of marrying age, must be wed within a year of the reading of the will, in order to inherit as a whole.'

Eve tucked her chin, blinked and blinked again. Had she *heard* the man correctly?

Their birthright would be *lost* if they weren't married before the year was out?

Married!

She laughed. The sound abrupt and startling the room, startling herself too.

'You think this is *funny*?' Rose fired as all eyes turned to the camera, to her.

'I think it's hilarious, Rose! I mean, come on, what century do you think we're in, Harrington?'

Rose lifted her hands. 'What am I missing?'

Did her sister *really* not get it?

'The land,' Matilda said quietly, 'is entailed to sons. If there is no son, the Waverly women can inherit—you, Eve and I—but only if all of us are married.'

Rose shot to her feet, pacing like a caged animal. 'That can't possibly be legal! Not in this day and age, surely!'

'Too right, it can't be,' Eve said, grateful that she wasn't the only one seeing this for what it was. Utterly farcical.

'It is…arcane,' Harrington said, 'but it has been a part of the lore of this land for several generations. So far as I see it, and so far as your father must have wanted, it stands.'

'How has this never come up before?' Rose said.

'Sons,' Matilda replied as Eve stared dumbfounded at the surreal scene playing out before her as if it were some movie and not reality. *Her* reality. 'Dad was an only child. Pop only had brothers, though one died of measles and the other drowned, meaning the farm passed straight to him. Waverlys have always been most excellent at having at least one strapping farm-loving son. Until us.'

Eve's stomach twisted. The idea that her mother

could have been deemed a failure for this too was an unwanted but very real thought.

'And what happens if we refuse to…marry,' Rose asked, staring Harrington down.

'If the condition is not met, the land goes back to the current head of the Garrison family. Clay Garrison.'

Rose scoffed. 'That double-dealing, underhand, two-faced old goat can't tell the back end of a bull from the front.'

'The son seems a reasonable sort—'

'*Lincoln…?* If he stopped partying long enough to even notice the level of responsibility coming his way…' Rose pressed her palms to her eyes. 'If our land, our home, the business that we've built fell into their hands, I—I can't even *think* it.'

'Don't waste your time worrying about it, Rose,' Eve said, finding her voice at last. 'Because it isn't going to happen. Not now. Not ever.'

Harrington cleared his throat. 'As it stands, unless all four of Holt Waverly's daughters are married within twelve months of the reading of this document—'

'Twelve months?' Rose shot back. 'But I can't… I'm not… I mean, none of us are even *seeing* anyone right now. Are we? Eve? Tilly?'

Never mind the months!

Eve's nose was right up against the screen. She *must* have misheard him this time. He said four, *four* daughters…

'Wait!' Matilda sat bolt upright, startling a dozing River. 'Back up a second. You said *four* daughters. There are only three of us.'

Then her sister's gaze drifted to the far corner of the room…a spot Eve couldn't see.

'Who are you?' Matilda said softly.

Who is who?

Everyone else was supposed to have left…

'Who are you talking to, Tilly? I can't see,' Eve said, desperate to turn the camera.

'Ana,' came a disembodied voice. Unsure. Hesitant. *Young*.

Harrington stood and stepped around the desk. 'Come forward, girl.'

Ana, who on earth was *Ana*?

Slowly, a dark-haired woman appeared in the bottom half of the screen and Eve felt the remaining blood drain from her face as her brain raced ahead for an answer.

Please let her be a distant cousin, an unexpected discovery on the depleted family tree, anything but…

'Anastasia,' Harrington said, 'this is Matilda Waverly. That there is Rose. And up on the screen is Evelyn. Girls, this is Anastasia Horvath.'

The stranger made the smallest sound, lifted her hand in what Eve took to be a wave. Matilda gestured back. Rose simply stared. And Eve… Eve didn't react because her insides were doing all the reacting for her, telling her before Harrington could who this girl was and why she was present…

'Ana here, is your father's daughter. Your half-sister. And therefore, according to your father's will, due an equal share in the estate. And equally beholden to the condition.'

Silence. No one moved. No one spoke. Eve couldn't. She was drowning in a sea of pain. All that hurt of old, the reason she'd left, the reason she never wanted to set foot on Garrison Downs again, the lie… She was staring at the product of that lie and she couldn't breathe.

'Impossible,' Matilda suddenly blurted.

Only Eve knew it wasn't.

It was entirely possible. Probable. True.

She fought for control, for something that wasn't the raging torrent within. Sense told her it wasn't this girl's fault that she existed. It wasn't this girl's fault that their father had been unfaithful. It wasn't this girl's fault that Eve had been forced to secrecy by her parents. That she'd been caught up in the lie, messed up by it, too.

But to learn that it wasn't just a fleeting affair, a thing of the past, a moment in time.

To learn that the consequences were as far-reaching as a child! A secret sister!

She couldn't bring herself to look at her. Harrington was still talking but Eve had heard enough. Too much!

She was going to vomit, she was sure of it. Right here, in her pristine glass-walled office for all her employees to witness.

'Rose?' Matilda started.

'Hang on.' Gripping the back of her chair, Rose

lifted her head to seek out Eve on the video screen and Eve knew she was piecing it all together. 'Evie…'

Not now, Rose, she silently pleaded, head shaking. *Not now.*

'Did you *know*? Is this why—'

'I have to go.'

She cut the call and the lid of her laptop in one, pressed her trembling palms into the top. Beyond the glass, her assistant Kim's eyes met hers.

You okay? she mouthed.

Eve could only stare and Kim was on her feet, inside her office and closing the shutters before anyone knew any different. 'I'll clear your schedule. You get yourself home.'

'No,' Eve whispered. 'I'm better off here.'

'You'll be better off at home.'

Home. London. Her apartment. Not Garrison Downs where her sisters were now coming to terms with this news. Her father's legacy as contentious and destructive as the man himself—a secret half-sister and a conditional bequest that sought to control them from the grave. To force them all into marriage, a bond he himself hadn't been able to honour.

The hypocrisy wasn't lost on her.

Well, you can forget it, dear old Dad.

She'd promised herself long ago that she would never tie herself to another, not in marriage and not in love, and she wasn't about to change that stance now. Not for anyone or anything, and least of all her liar of a father.

But she wouldn't see her sisters lose their birth-right either.

The condition had to go, and she would see it gone. Woe betide *anyone* who stood in her way.

CHAPTER ONE

A few miles out from Marni,
South Australian Outback,
September

IF SOMEONE HAD told Eve three months ago, she'd be taking a three-month sabbatical and returning to Garrison Downs, she'd have laughed in their face. On both counts.

Work was her life.

And the Downs was her living hell.

Yet here she was in the back of a cab heading into Marni, the nearest Outback town to the god-forsaken place.

Far enough away from the station to hide a little longer, but close enough to feel its proximity like an invisible noose around her neck.

She rubbed at her nape. Her hand coming away damp. Didn't matter that the car's air con was dialled up, her stress levels had her overheating from the inside out. She checked the temperature display—a cool sixteen degrees—she could hardly ask her driver to lower it again. The look he'd sent her as he'd tugged his sweater on the last time she'd asked told her she was mad enough.

Instead, she pulled out her laptop, aiming for distraction. What she got was a streak of goosebumps to accompany the clammy sheen, because staring back at her was the image that had triggered this mad dash across the world.

Matilda. Her little sister. A bride!

And not just any bride, a blushing bona fide *princess* bride!

Eve wasn't sure what shocked her more, the fact that she'd married royalty or the fact she was married at all!

Oh, Matilda *claimed* she was in love. Claimed she was happy. Swore it had nothing to do with the blasted will and everything to do with her heart.

But Tilly, dear sweet adventurous Tilly...?

She stared at the photograph. A feature of the official royal press release showing Matilda with her husband in all their wedding finery, but it was their smiles and the look in their eyes that caught at Eve most.

Was it possible? Had her sister really found true love? A real-life fairy-tale castle for a home too?

She choked on a laugh. It was surreal. As surreal as the situation it left her and the rest of her sisters in...

She couldn't help Tilly now, she'd made her bed and, as her sister had pointed out on their latest call, she was very happy rolling around in it. *Not* the image Eve had wanted but she'd smiled despite herself. Her sister's joy too infectious to resist.

But if that joy were to expire, then Eve would be there to help pick up the pieces. For it didn't matter how happy Tilly looked right now, how happy a couple they seemed…how would they be a year or two or ten down the line when life tested them? What then?

And as for her other sisters, the pressure…

Three months she'd spent trying to find a way out of the condition. Three long months of speaking to lawyers in the states, going around in circles and getting nowhere. Refusing to admit defeat and feeling it all the same…

She scrolled down the article until the small headshot of her father came into view. As if the world needed a reminder of who their father was and who they were by association…

Eve swallowed the rising sickness and slammed the laptop shut.

How could he do this to them when his own marriage had been such a sham?

To think her parents' love affair had been lauded across Australia, their famed whirlwind romance leading to a lasting Happy Ever After with three daughters and a glorious happy home, a tale to be celebrated.

And it had all been a lie…

At least her sisters now knew the truth, she wasn't alone in shouldering it any more, but the clock was ticking. They had nine months to wed

or get out of this mess. And get out of it she would.
For Rose's sake.

Garrison Downs might be a distant memory for
Eve, but for her big sister, it was her home, her live-
lihood, her everything. Eve had no desire to return,
let alone own any part of it. And Matilda now had
a whole kingdom of her own to go at.

As for Anastasia, heaven knew what she made
of it all and Eve didn't want to care. Ana was a reminder of the affair Eve wanted to forget. So, no,
what mattered was Rose and securing it for Rose.

But *marriage*?

The idea made her shudder, fear setting in. Because if Matilda was already married, what was
to stop Rose doing the same? Throwing away her
life, her happiness, because she couldn't see another way out.

Or Ana for that matter. She might not know the
girl but no woman deserved to be chained to a man
because of their father's screwed-up legacy.

One of them had to keep a clear head and she
feared she was the only one with a heart detached
enough to do it.

Home of the Harringtons, Marni,
South Australian Outback,
September

'You'll need to keep a close eye on those Waverly
girls.'

'Women, Dad. They're women.' Nate turned from

the study window where he'd been watching his mother tend to her vegetable patch, preferring the sight of her presence out there over the company this side of the glass. 'Last I checked, they're all in their twenties now.'

His father gave a rattling cough, one frail hand trembling in his direction as he shifted in his seat behind the desk. 'Don't be so pedantic.'

Nate held his tongue. He didn't have the taste for a fight. Not when he was still coming to terms with the sight of his father like this. Broken. Weak.

His thick dark hair streaked with grey and thinning on top. Skin an unhealthy shade of pale and hazel eyes, dim and yellow, obscured by small round spectacles. Spectacles he'd never needed before. Just as he hadn't needed the walking stick… or for his son to hurry home and take on the family firm.

He stifled a derisive laugh. *Needed.* By his father of all people.

There'd been a time when Nate would have cherished that call. Cherished the moment his father acknowledged that he was good enough for Harrington Law, good enough for him.

But that call hadn't come because George Harrington finally thought his son was good enough, it had come because he was desperate. Forced into retirement on the grounds of ill health, a move considered long overdue by everyone else but the man himself, and he had no one else to ask.

'They'll always be Holt's girls to me,' his father

said, garnering strength from somewhere. Grief for his oldest client? Concern for the women now without their father? 'And they need looking out for.'

And where was this concern for Nate growing up?

If only his father had shown a fraction of it, how different things could've been. Maybe he wouldn't have left for Sydney and set up on his own. Maybe they would've had a relationship, something that wasn't this…

'Looking out for them would be seeing this arcane stipulation thrown out.'

'That arcane stipulation is there for a reason.'

'So you say…'

'It's for their benefit as much as the land.'

He widened his gaze, his nod slow as he drawled, 'Right.'

'Don't mock me, son.'

'I'm not mocking you. I'm mocking the condition.'

'The condition, as executor of the will, you're now responsible for overseeing.'

'Whatever you say, Dad.'

Nate went back to the window, buried his hands in his jeans as he watched his mother fill her basket with fresh pickings. Her floral dress as bright and summery as her smile had been when he'd arrived. Her relief to have him home as obvious as her joy. It twisted him up inside. Guilt for not coming home more. Guilt for not wanting to be here now.

'You're not filling me with confidence.'

Nate's bitterness rolled with his laugh. 'When did I ever, Dad?'

He kept his eyes on his mother, seeking her out as he had as a child, when he'd needed the calm, the warmth, some affection…often finding her doing the same, tending to the garden or cooking up something delicious in the kitchen. Carving out her own space within the home that had always felt broken to Nate.

No wonder he'd migrated towards her. He was his mother through and through. Blond hair, blue eyes, an easy smile and ready zest for life…something his father had done his best to stifle growing up. More work, less play. A hard word spoken worth a thousand soft. How his mother coped, Nate hadn't a clue.

'This is important, son. You need—'

'What I *need* is for you to let me do my job,' Nate interjected. 'I said I'd come home. I said I'd take on the firm. I said I'd see this job done and I will. I don't have to like it.'

His father muttered something incoherent, but Nate was done with the discussion. He was done with the entire visit. He didn't want to be here. For as much as he loved his mother, he couldn't bear being in the same room as his father. The man's presence enough to see the inferiority complex Nate grew up with creep back in. Weaving like a vine through everything he'd achieved, suffocating and smothering until it no longer existed.

Didn't matter that he'd made youngest equity

partner his global law firm had ever seen, his pent-house overlooking Sydney harbour as sought after as his legal clout, his father still had the ability to make him weak.

'Just tell me one thing,' he said, 'how did it get to this point? Holt must have realised the implication of having no sons...'

'He never raised it with me.'

'And you, *you* didn't think to raise it with him?' His frown was sharp...whatever he thought of his father, he'd never doubted the lawyer in him. 'Or does the idea of four women being forced into marriage sit well with you?'

Another cough racked his body and Nate bit back a curse. Hating that he cared.

It was time to go. He'd done what he set out to, collected the keys for his father's office in town—now his—and arranged for the boxes of paperwork he had squirrelled away here to be shipped back. He could leave.

So why were his feet still rooted?

The answer walked past the window, her eyes lighting on his and her smile worth every chilling second in his father's company. He waved.

'He will have had his reasons.'

'Reasons he never shared because you failed to raise it?'

'Holt knew that document inside out, to raise it would be to question his judgement.'

'But as his lawyer...?'

'As his lawyer—' He broke off, coughing harder,

unrelenting. He beat his chest, struggling to catch his breath and Nate stepped forward, panic rising.

'Dad—'

'Don't!' His father urged him back. 'Don't you dare pander to me.'

Pander? Nate shook his head. Frustrated by his father's reaction, frustrated even more by the concern he couldn't quash. 'I wouldn't dream of it.'

'As his lawyer and his friend, I respected his wishes.'

'And you honestly think he wished for this?'

'I think he wished for his daughters to have someone to share the vast responsibility of Garrison Downs with, just as he had Rosamund. She was his rock.'

'How can you say that when you know of the affair?'

Nate had been thrown by the discovery. Up until recently, he, like everyone else, had believed the idyllic fairy tale that was the great romance of Aussie tycoon Holt Waverly and English socialite Rosamund Lavigne. Nate had believed the man to have everything he wanted for himself one day. A career, a wife, children, a happy home perfectly in balance. Not like his childhood. Not like this home.

But then it hadn't been quite so perfect, after all. Anastasia's existence proved that.

'Granted, they had their challenges in the early days, when the girls were young and Rosamund was unwell, and neither knew what was wrong.'

'And what was wrong?'

His father gave him a peculiar look. 'It's not my place to say. Just take my word for it, the affair was short-lived. Their marriage survived and their love was stronger for it.'

Nate shook his head. 'If you say so...'

'I do. Though...' His father hesitated, his gaze drifting to the window and giving Nate the impression he was losing him to his thoughts. Eventually, he said, 'Truth be told, I think Holt hoped the bequest would unite them.'

'Unite them?'

'The sisters.' He met Nate's confused frown. 'Aside from Rose and Matilda, they live very separate lives and I think he feared that would never change. He saw Rose as too married to the land. Evelyn never coming home. Matilda never leaving. And as for Anastasia, he may have regretted the affair, but he loved her and what better way to ingratiate her into the family she's never known than to permit this?'

Nate was reluctant to admit it, but there was something in that...not a lot, but something.

'It may not be fair and could be deemed sexist and antiquated but—'

'There's no may or could about it, Dad.'

His father gave a heavy sigh, removed his glasses and rubbed a weary hand across his brow. 'But it's how Holt left things and I need you to do this for me. After that, you can do whatever you wish. Go back to Sydney and your fancy city life, forget all about Marni and what it means to be a part of this community…'

Nate would contradict him if he thought his father would hear him. Experience told him he wouldn't.

'Hell, maybe you'll decide to stay and make something of my legacy as I'm sure Holt's daughters will do with his…your mother would certainly like that.'

He scoffed and his father's gaze collided with his.

'Please…' he clenched his fist upon the desk '…do this one thing for me and make me proud?'

'Proud?' Nate choked out.

'Is that too much to ask?'

After thirty-five years of trying, it was.

'Son?'

Nate shook his head. He could fight back, but what was the point? His father wouldn't change and he wasn't the boy desperate for his father's affection any more.

'I'll do my job. No more, no less. Now, if that's everything I'll be off…'

He headed for the door and his father shot up faster than he would have thought possible. 'You're leaving?'

'I think I've served my purpose by being here, don't you?'

He paused to give his father his full attention and the man studied him back, his gaze making Nate's skin prickle and his ears burn. 'Your mother was hoping you'd stay for dinner.'

His mother... There he went again, putting it all on her.

'And you?' he dared to press. 'Were you hoping the same?'

'I'm sure we can put our differences aside for one meal.'

He shook his head, huffed out, 'Not today.'

He tugged open the door with more force than it required and fought the urge to slam it shut behind him. He took a breath, waited for his pulse to ease before heading off in search of his mother.

He didn't want to upset her with his mood, and yet upsetting her was par for the course whenever he and his hypercritical father were in the same room.

'Sweetheart!'

As if sensing his distress, she appeared in the hallway, hope alive in her sparkling blue eyes. He forced a smile.

'Mum...'

'I was coming to see if you'll be stopping for dinner. I've just picked the most glorious-looking carrots and—'

'Sunday, Mum. I'll come on Sunday.' He gave her a kiss to the cheek to soften the blow. He needed to get over this initial visit, then he could stomach food in his father's company. 'You know how much I love your roast.'

'But you can come Sunday, too. Really, darling, I don't know why you're not staying here...' Though the hesitation in her gaze told him she knew well enough. 'We haven't seen you in so long and your room is all ready for you.'

'Another time…'

'Let the boy go, Sue-Ellen,' came his father's stern command, and his mother's eyes widened, still pleading.

'I'll see you Sunday, Mum. I'm back for good, remember.'

And ignoring his father, he gave her another peck to the cheek and strode out.

Plucking his helmet off the back off his Harley, he shoved it on and mounted the bike. Started the engine. Gave it a hearty, head-clearing rev and rode off. Blasting his father out as he headed deeper into town.

Perched on the edge of a desert, Marni had the essentials—a shop, a school, a tiny cinema and pubs. Lots of pubs and one with rooms. His home until he could find somewhere to rent. And he was sure he'd find the company far more to his liking there. Company that he hadn't enjoyed in too long.

Sydney had its perks but the people…no one could beat the laid-back scene of the Outback. Give him jeans over a suit any day, preferably with a coldie and his evening was made.

And that was just what he needed to see off the remnants of his father.

The pub, the chilled beer and the…the *company*?

He slowed the bike as he neared the quirky century-old pub, its single-storey sandstone walls, corrugated-iron roof and wide shady veranda, a rustic welcome sight. The country music and cheer spilling out of the open windows and doors inviting too. But amongst the trucks and the motorcycles lined up outside sat a sleek black town car.

At least it would have been sleek before the red dust of the Outback had given it an extra layer. As for the woman stepping out of it…

She had the grace of a swan and dressed the part too. White flowing skirt, sleeveless white blouse, white heels that threatened to touch the sky and hair as gold as the sun starting to dip behind the horizon.

No one wore white in the Outback. Not if they wanted it to stay white.

He chuckled. So much for leaving the city behind…

CHAPTER TWO

EVE STEPPED OUT of the cab, stretched her travel-weary limbs and almost recoiled back into the air-conditioned cabin.

It wasn't as though she'd forgotten how oppressive the heat of the Outback could be, but it was spring. *Not* the height of summer. And the sun was already low in the sky, its amber glow casting shadows over the shack-cum-pub that was to be her home for the night.

As a child, Eve had strolled past The Royal Oak many times but never once had she ventured through the double swing doors. She couldn't say the music and raucous laughter spilling through the shuttered windows were encouraging her to do so now either but, as it was the only place in town with rooms to rent, she had no choice.

Pushing her sunglasses into her hair, she wrinkled her nose. It would be an experience. An experience that beat flying straight to the station where Rose and the pain of old were waiting for her.

Eight years it had been.

Eight years since she'd last visited as an outsider

at her own mother's funeral…she pressed a hand to her chest, suppressed the rising shiver.

'That's everything,' her driver said, setting her luggage down. 'You want me to take them in, ma'am?'

Her mouth twitched. Ma'am? Really?

'No. Thank you.' She hitched her handbag under her arm. 'I can take it from here.'

'Fair enough.' The chap frowned at the building and scratched the back of his head. Probably wondering what a woman like her was doing in a place like this. Not that she could blame him. She looked like the outsider she was and that suited her fine. She didn't want to belong. Marni was her past and the sooner she could put it in the rear-view mirror again, the better.

He dipped his cap and drove off, a cloud of red dust kicking up in his wake, and she flapped a hand. Coughed. Whether it was really in her lungs or not, the pesky red stuff was everywhere, clinging to every surface and now her white linen culottes too.

She grimaced and flicked at her thigh, creating streaks out of the tiny specks and making it so much worse.

And why did that feel like some omen?

Ignoring the foolish thought, she threw her travel bag over her shoulder and grabbed the recessed suitcase handle, pressed the button to extend it and strode forth—promptly falling back again.

What in the…?

She eyed the unmoving handle, the stubborn suitcase with it. Rocked the entire thing side to side and tried again, her cool rapidly depleting in the cloying heat. There was no breeze, no reprieve. And that wasn't all the years in London talking, this smacked of a heatwave. Just what she needed when she was so far out of her comfort zone already.

'Come! On!'

She yanked at her case, her outburst drowned out by the roar of an approaching motorcycle. Its pace slowed and her neck prickled. The last thing she needed was some biker coming to her aid or, worse, sitting back as an amused audience to her plight.

The engine cut and she kept her gaze averted. Tried every angle, every move, her other bags threatening to hit the dirt.

'Need a hand, miss?'

Ma'am. Miss. What she wouldn't give to have a good old British luv thrown at her!

The bike creaked as he dismounted, boots hitting earth.

'I'm fine!' she hurried out, staring at the unresponsive case as if she could murder it with her mind. 'Thank you!'

'Suit yourself,' came the deep burr, though she sensed his eyes still on her. Probably as bemused and bewildered as the cab driver.

She ignored the prickling awareness running down her spine. Awareness and perspiration—*ew*!

Lifting one foot and bracing it against the case, she gave the handle a hefty tug, so hefty it almost sent her toppling back as, finally, it came loose. With a triumphant harrumph, she moved before she could appear any more inept and pushed her way through the doors into…into…

Oh, dear God.

The country music vibrated through the floor-boards into her dainty stilettos as she breathed in the stench of beer and…*cowboy*—the only suitable descriptor for the masculine tinge in the air.

All around her, Outback paraphernalia cluttered every wall. Beer bottles and mats, cans, street signs, local notices, trophies, awards. You couldn't see the ceiling for Akubras, well-worn and well-stained. Her nose wrinkled further…if it kept on going it would disappear inside her head.

And that was when she felt it, every eye in the room on her.

Locals who hadn't so much as turned her way, but she sensed their gazes shift beneath the rims of their hats as they assessed the stranger in their midst. Because no one would know who she was. No matter the fame of her family, she bore no resemblance to the girl who'd left all those years ago. The alias she'd used to book the room ensuring she flew under the radar of the Marni gossip train and local media for as long as possible.

She straightened and teetered forward, careful not to lose a heel in the craggy floor, and cleared her dust-filled throat. A drink. She'd have a cool drink and then she'd… She peered over the counter at the line of fridges and fell at the first hurdle.

Did this place not serve *wine*? They were in South Australia, for goodness' sake!

'G'day, darl.' The bartender approached, his age impossible to decipher with a bushy beard hiding half his face and an impressive hat-shaped wedge in his hatless hair. 'What can I do you for?'

She checked out the other patrons beneath her lashes. Everyone clutched a beer.

'Do you have… Prosecco?'

He arched a brow. 'Prosecco?'

She nodded—*You're the customer, stick to your guns.*

'Right, you are. Ey, Betty, love! Get this one a glass of that bubbly stuff you like.'

A woman appeared from the back, brown hair swinging in a ponytail, shirt tied in a knot across her midriff, bootcut jeans and a wide smile.

'Grab yourself a seat, darl, I'll bring it over.'

She hesitated, looking around. She didn't fancy taking up one of the huge barrels acting as tables in the centre of the room, so she headed to the end of the bar. Out of the way. Set herself down beside an Akubra-wearing longhorn skull, a companion long past judgement, and propped her handbag on the bar just as her phone buzzed from within. She slotted her sunglasses away and pulled out her phone to find a message from Rose.

Landed yet?

She flinched. There was no softness, no kiss, which Eve was sure she'd add for Tilly. Not that she could blame Rose. Her sister had taken it hard when

she'd left for the UK with no explanation, taken it
ever harder when she'd stood by their grandparents for Mum's funeral and then failed to return
for Dad's. And though Eve knew Rose had pieced
some of it together, they had yet to have *that* conversation...

She kept her response equally brief.

Here. Safe and Sound. I'll be with you tomorrow.

Sure you don't want me to come get you?

Eve clenched her teeth. And spend a full hour's
car journey in confined quarters suffering in awkward silence, or, worse, battling it out?

No, thanks. You have the station to run. I'll find
my own way.

She then texted Gran to let her know she'd arrived safe. Since her grandfather had died six years
ago, Granny Lavigne had transferred all her concern Eve's way and Eve often wondered how much
of it was regret over the past and a wish for a better future, one in which she could embrace all her
granddaughters again.

Another good reason for Eve to be here and help
bridge that gap.

Another huge feat.

'Here you go, darl.' Betty set her drink down
with a bowl of crackling and a wink. 'You look
like you could do with it, honey.'

Do with it? Do with what?

'I wouldn't take offence.'

She started—that voice, the biker…oh, dear God.

She lifted her drink, an *actual* flute, and gulped down a mouthful without tasting. Then, because social etiquette dictated, she forced a smile and turned to face…to face…

Chris Flipping Hemsworth!

Okay, so not really Chris, but maybe his secret brother. She had a secret Ana after all.

'Hi. The name's Nate.'

He offered out a hand—a strong, super-capable hand. Attached to a strong, super-capable forearm, well honed and well inked. Not that she could make out enough of the design before it disappeared beneath the rolled-back cuff to his black shirt.

Eve swallowed air. Ignored the hand and the arm.

'Hi.'

If her body wasn't already cooking in the Aussie heat, her neglected libido would have it stoked to a flurry of flames. No bushy beard here. He sported the very definition of designer stubble cut to enhance a masculine jaw, cheekbones even she would kill for and lips so full and captivating, they made one think of kissing.

Kissing and hot summer nights.

And, jeez, Louise, give it up.

She went back to her drink, took a gulp.

'No name?'

She flicked him a look. His brows were drawn together over eyes that were as bright and as deep as the azure blue sea, though that breath-stealing grin remained wide. She took another swig and told her ovaries to douse the fuse.

'I don't make a habit of giving my name to strangers.'

He chuckled, the sound low and rumbling its way through her. 'Mind if I sit?'

She managed a shrug, crossing her legs and angling away as he slid onto the stool beside her. If only her eyes could be as easily diverted. Instead they drifted his way. Still attractive, still making her blood zing. Windswept hair, overlong, somewhere between blond and brown and streaked with sun-kissed gold.

He leaned into the bar, those ink-adorned forearms flexing with the move, his denim jeans stretching over thick, strong thighs...

He gestured to Betty behind the bar and she came over with a bottle of beer and the obligatory wink.

Either he came here often enough for Betty to know his order, or she'd taken a wild guess. But then Eve was the only one without a beer, it was hardly a leap. She went to take another sip and realised she was out already.

'If you're hoping that'll quench your thirst, you'll be disappointed.'

She sent him a well-rehearsed, unimpressed glance. 'Is that so?'

'Only a coldie can hit that spot...'

His eyes flitted to her chest, where she knew a

trickle of perspiration had disappeared down the V of her blouse…and why did it feel as if he'd touched her there too?

She squeezed her legs against the sudden pang.

'Unless…' His eyes sparked with challenge, his mouth lifting to one side.

'Unless what?'

She wet her lips, eyed the condensation on his bottle as he raised it to his lips and her disloyal mouth salivated, her eyes drinking in the motion. His mouth against the bottle, the broadness of his neck, the bob to his Adam's apple, all the way down to the hint of another tattoo where his shirt fell open at the collar…

'Unless you're too fancy for a good old-fashioned beer?'

She shimmied in her seat, righted her shoulders in indignation. 'Not in the slightest.'

His hypnotic blue gaze danced. 'No?'

'I just don't think alcohol is the right drink to quench one's thirst.'

Oh, how prim and proper you sound—Granny Lavigne would be so proud.

'Hence the…' He gestured to her empty glass.

'I was about to order a water.'

'Right,' he drawled, 'course you were.'

She bit back a stubborn retort. Why was she letting him get to her?

He isn't getting to you, he's exciting you! Giving you a buzz you haven't felt outside work in far too long and it's freaking you out.

Hardly surprising when he was so different from the men she dated in London. All designer suits, clean-shaven and careful with every word. Always the gentleman too. Not that he wasn't but…

'Someone say water?'

Betty popped a bottle in front of her and Eve gave a surprised, 'Thank you.'

More grateful that she'd saved her from her rambling thoughts than the drink itself.

'Not a problem, darl. Can I get you another fizz?'

'Please.'

Biker smirked and before she could stop herself, Eve called her back. 'Actually, I'll get…' she grasped for the name of a beer, *any* beer, her jet-lagged brain drawing a blank '…same as what he's having.'

Another ovary-rousing chuckle. 'Don't change your order on my account.'

'Don't flatter yourself, buddy.' A defiant tilt of the chin, her gaze on the barmaid. 'I don't do anything I don't want to.'

'And you want a beer?'

His deep Australian drawl was too damned appealing, as was the pull of his tease and scepticism…

She turned to face him, all fired up. 'Too right I do.'

Said drink appeared beside her and, without looking, she picked it up, arched her head back and drank. Every…last…drop.

Take that, buddy.

* * *

Nate watched her neck the beer. Head thrown back, golden hair almost touching the bar, glossy lips wrapped around the bottle as her elegant throat bobbed with every swallow... *Holy mother of...*

With a satisfied 'Ah', she righted the bottle and herself. Eyes sparkling, lips damp, she checked the empty contents. 'You're right, that did touch the spot.'

'You've done that before.'

'Might have.'

Her eyes widened and she tucked in her chin, pressed the backs of her fingers to her lips as she contained a definite burp.

'Excuse me,' and then she laughed. Surprised, horrified, amused. Likely all the above. 'I don't normally do that.'

'Laugh or belch?'

She laughed some more, blushed too. The flush of colour making her blue eyes shine and softening every hard edge she'd been projecting until now. She uncrossed her legs, eased a little closer and he realised he was wrong earlier; it wasn't a skirt but wide-leg pants. The fabric as delicate as she'd first appeared.

But this woman was far from delicate. She was a force of nature, and he was loving every second of their interaction, rebukes and all.

'Actually, come to think of it...' she sobered, as though remembering what she was about '...both.'

'And that's a mighty shame.'

She gave him the side eye, a look he was coming to enjoy more than he should. Part flirtation, part rack off. 'You want more belching?'

He grinned. 'I want more laughing but if it takes some belching first, it's a price I'm willing to pay.'

Her mouth twitched at the corners. 'How very accommodating.'

'Not something I'm used to hearing, but I'll take it.'

She looked at him properly now, twisting in her chair. Her knee brushed against his thigh and his skin came alive, a tantalising warmth pulsing its way straight to his groin. He took up his beer. Made it appear all causal when he desperately needed the cool distraction…especially when he could sense her cogs working overtime.

'What?'

'You're right, you don't *look* the accommodating type.'

'No?' He narrowed his gaze, lowered his beer. 'How *do* I look?'

She nipped her lip. 'You really want to know?'

Was she *flirting* with him now? Or was that just wishful thinking on his part?

'I wouldn't ask if I didn't.' Though maybe he should reconsider because that look in her eye was taking this somewhere he hadn't expected…somewhere he doubted she had either.

'You look the exact opposite.'

'Which would be?'

'Unmoving. Unobliging.' She leaned closer with

each descriptor, and he supped his beer again, finding safety in the distraction. 'Inflexible. Stubborn.'

Definitely flirting, and he was definitely liking it.

'Hard.'

He nearly spat his beer.

'Well, you did ask,' she said, throwing back some water.

'And do you always say what you think?'

She shrugged. 'When it suits me or the task at hand.'

'And is that what I am, some task at hand?'

Her blue eyes pinned him. 'Would you *like* to be my task at hand?'

Woah, this was going too far, too fast, yet he had no desire to make it stop. And clearly, neither did she.

'You're not from around here, are you?'

And just like that, he'd stamped on the brake. He might as well have thrown ice over her for the sudden chill in the air. He was torn between changing topic and asking what was wrong.

The former was the least contentious, especially when they were nothing more than strangers. But the latter was what he really wanted so he opted for something in between.

'Sorry, but those shoes gave you away. Reckon they'll do you some mischief in these parts...'

She pursed her lips, her eyes coming alive again.

'Then there's your accent... English if I'm not mistaken.'

'Very perceptive.'

'Perceptive,' he drawled, raising his brows. 'I'll add that to accommodating. My positive traits are growing.'

She was smiling now. Enough for him to bite the bullet and say, 'So tell me, just what is a woman like you doing in a place like this?'

'Would you believe me if I said I was on holiday?'

'Alone?'

'Who says I'm alone?'

'The luggage at your feet and no companion to be seen.'

'Who says I'm not meeting somcone?'

'Are you?'

'Might be.'

'Lucky someone.'

She laughed, her eyes sparkling like Sydney Harbour on a bright summer's day. 'Are you always so smooth?'

'Smooth, perceptive, *and* accommodating. I'm winning today.'

She shook her head. 'Winning indeed. And no.' She pulled a strand of hair from her lip, its glossy fullness holding his eye a second longer than was wise. 'I'm not meeting anyone. I'm here because…'

She blew out a breath, giving herself cheeks like a hamster—not something she'd appreciate hearing, he was sure, but adorable all the same.

'Because?' he pressed when she didn't continue, her gaze falling to the empty beer bottle as she rocked it against the bar.

'Because I have a family issue to take care of and...' she cast her gaze over the room '...it's complicated.'

'In my experience, families always are.'

'You too?'

He took a swig of beer and sucked the air through his teeth. 'Let's just say my father and I don't get along.'

'Now there's a tale I understand...' She clinked her bottle against his, warming to him again. 'What is it with yours?'

'Aside from me being invisible to him growing up?' He doused the bitterness with another sip. 'Nothing I ever did was good enough.'

'Let me guess...' her eyes were soft with understanding, the kind that came from experience '...another sibling steal the limelight?'

'No. No siblings. Just me. I guess you did though.'

She nodded.

'How many siblings stole your stage?'

Her mouth twisted. 'Too many.'

'Sisters, brothers?'

'All sisters.'

He winced. 'So what are you? The eldest, the youngest, middle...'

'Second eldest.'

'Forever in your older sister's shadow?' he surmised. 'Or overlooked for the younger, the needier?'

'You really are quite astute...'

'So you've said. Perceptive, remember.'

'For a man, it's quite refreshing.'

'And I'm sure I should be accusing you of sexism now.'

'So why aren't you?'

'Because I'm too interested in what makes you tick.'

She shook her head, her laugh more strained now. 'Are we really doing this?'

'Doing what?'

'Having a dose of family therapy at the bar?'

'Better some therapy than none.'

She stared at him. 'Are you always like this with people you've just met?'

'When they interest me.'

She gave a soft chuckle, held his eye as she took a swig of water, then, 'If you really must know, my older sister is my father in female form, she could do no wrong. My younger sister is all sunshine and light, and again…'

'She could do no wrong,' he said with her. 'And your other?'

Her jaw pulsed, her eyes evading him as she muttered something that sounded much like, 'Damned if I know.'

'I'm sorry?'

'Nothing.'

'Let me guess…' he smiled softly '…it's complicated.'

'Got it in one. So what was your father's excuse?'

'He was married to his work.'

'Something else that sounds familiar…'

'You too? What does he do?'

'Did.' She swallowed, her jaw pulsing again. 'He's dead.'

He stilled, his hand reaching between them. 'I'm sorry, I didn't—'

'I'm not.' Though it came out forced, too quick, too learned.

'In that case, I'm even more sorry.'

'Don't be, I lost my father long before he left this world.'

Her eyes blazed but beneath the fire there was pain. Unresolved. Potent.

'Want to talk about it?'

She cocked a brow at him, scoffed, 'No.'

'Okay, "want" is the wrong word to use, how about "need"? Because I'm willing to listen. No judgment. All ears.'

'Nice try, but I'm not all mouth so...' She sipped her water, her mouth very much drawing him in as she dismissed the turn in conservation as readily as they'd hit on it.

What was it about this woman that made him want to go deeper, to dig beneath the cool facade to the woman beneath?

When was the last time he'd felt such a pull...?

Had he ever?

He forced himself to relax back on his stool, to ease up. If she didn't want to talk about it, it wasn't right for him to push it. 'I rarely talk about my father either.'

'And your mother?' she asked, coming back to him a little.

'She's an entirely different breed from him.' He smiled. Thoughts of his mum making the gesture easy. 'Soft, loving, always willing to listen. Always nagging me to come home too.'

She blinked, her gaze falling away but not before he swore he caught a tear. 'That's nice.'

'It has its moments,' he said, carefully. 'What about yours?'

Though he sensed her answer in the melancholic air, whatever had tainted her relationship with her father, it didn't seem to extend to her mother because there was no bitterness now, only sadness. 'Also, dead.'

He reached out again but this time he covered her hand, warm and soft beneath his own. 'I'm sorry.'

She took a shallow breath, gave the tiniest of shrugs. 'It was a long time ago now. I don't know why it hurts so much.'

'She was your mother. It's always going to hurt.'

'She was my mother but…'

She slipped her hand from his, gripped it in her lap.

'But?'

She gave a rapid shake of her head, rolled her shoulders back, parking whatever it was some place deep and not to be examined. 'It's…'

'Complicated?' he finished for her.

'And you know…' she murmured, her eyes lifting to his, their sudden spark catching him unawares, 'I'd much rather talk about these.'

She reached out to lightly trace the tattoo on

one arm, her touch firing up the nerve-endings beneath and making the muscle twitch, his entire body tense.

She snatched her hand back, making a fist. 'I'm sorry. I shouldn't have—'

He shook his head. 'Not at all. I just wasn't expecting it.'

Not the delicate touch or the way it powered through him, coiling through his core. Making him want more. So much more.

'How about I trade you background on my tattoos for whatever has that frown forming just there?' He gestured to the crease between her brows, resisting the urge to reach out and smooth it away with his thumb.

'It's an interesting proposition,' she murmured, tilting her head to the side.

'An agreeable one?'

'I'm not so sure…how do I know if it's a fair trade?'

'You don't.'

'You're not selling it very well.'

'On the contrary, I'm rousing your curiosity.'

She laughed, shook her head. 'Is that so?'

'And you seem like a woman who thrives off taking the odd risk.'

She laughed harder. 'At work perhaps, but in my personal life…'

'In your personal life they reap the biggest reward.'

Her lashes fluttered. 'Now I know you're talking nonsense.'

'And you're a woman who avoids talking about anything deep and meaningful so…?'

'You think you have me sussed.'

'I think I have a fair idea of the woman you are and we haven't even exchanged names.'

'Oh, we did… You're Nate.'

'And you are?'

She gave him a cocky grin. 'Doesn't my lack of identity make this connection all the more thrilling?'

'Thrilling for you, yes.' And he had to admit, he liked her putting words to it. A connection. It meant she felt it too. This intense attraction that had his body so attuned to hers while their verbal sparring had his head firing too. 'But it puts me at a disadvantage.'

Her smile widened. 'Just where I like you.'

'Beautiful *and* power-hungry. That's quite the combination.'

She leaned a little closer. 'In my line of work, it pays to be both.'

'And what line is that?' he pressed, sensing he was close to learning something real.

'Public relations, advertising, marketing people's wares…'

It certainly fit the image.

'Any hobbies on the side?'

'Just work.'

'No husband, no partner…'

'No time for a man.'

He cocked a brow. 'Don't you ever get lonely?'

'I don't have time to get lonely.'

'Yet here you are, in a bar...'

'I'm on a three-month sabbatical.'

And she didn't sound happy about it.

'Already missing it?'

'Quite.'

'Now you remind me of my father.'

'Ouch.'

She was teasing, he wasn't. The similarity should have been enough to see him giving his goodbyes... instead his butt was rooted, his body leaning closer.

'So, do I get a name?'

She pursed her lips, narrowed her gaze...

'What name would you give me?'

'Oh, no, you don't.' He eased back. 'I'm not playing this game.'

'Why not?'

'Too much at stake.'

'How so?'

'I give you a name you don't like and you wrinkle your nose like you did when you stepped out of that cab back there. Or the opposite happens, I give you a name that implies I find you attractive and send you running. There's no right answer and, thus, I cannot win.'

She laughed softly. 'You're probably right.'

'So?'

'It's Eve.'

'Eve?'

Her gaze flicked over the room. 'Just Eve.'

'Well, *just* Eve, you have improved my day a hundred times over and for that, I thank you.'

'No thank you necessary, you've done the same for me. I've dreaded this trip and I was counting down the seconds until I can escape again. Meeting you has put a temporary pause on that ticking clock.'

He frowned at the depth of feeling behind her words, at how much she hated it here... Or hated what had brought her here?

'What's with the frown?' she purred.

'I'm disappointed you're in such a hurry to leave.'

'Why? Are you sticking around because, pardon me for being so blunt, you don't look like you're from around here either?'

'I don't?'

'You're a little rough around the edges, granted, but your beard is too groomed, your accent too city-like...'

'Very perceptive,' he said, throwing her own compliment back at her and coaxing out another smile.

'Something else we have in common. So...' She tilted her head once more. 'You didn't answer my question—are you sticking around?'

'If things work out how I plan, yes.'

'Things with your family or...'

'Family and work.'

'And what plans are those?'

'I thought you didn't want to sweat the serious stuff, right now?'

She gave him a slow smile. 'Okay. Tattoos it is...'

And then her hands were back on him, her fingers tracing the black ink, and it was all he could do to keep his cool and concentrate on the words passing through her lips rather than what he wanted to do with them.

'Tell me about this one...'

He shifted in his seat, told his body to behave. 'You like him?'

'Him?' She raised both brows. 'I don't know, I can't see *him* properly.'

'Is that you asking for a better look?'

'Maybe.'

He chuckled low in his throat, placed his beer down and rolled back his cuff. She lowered her gaze, eyes distinctly hungry, their heat working its way through him too as she reached out to lift his arm closer and gave a breathy, 'Oh!'

She might as well have had an orgasm and been blissful in its aftermath for the image that simple sound evoked. Did she have any idea what she was doing to him? Her appreciation. Her extended touch. Her blazing blue eyes.

'That's impressive.' She stroked her fingers over his skin, tracing the intricate sketch of a wolf emerging from a forest, one paw reaching down his arm.

'Not what my father thought,' he said, recalling the showdown with a grim smile. 'Nor my mother, though she came around eventually.'

'How old were you when you had it done?'

'Eighteen. A rebellious move born of a rebellious teen.'

'Your father's words?'

'Words of that ilk, yes.'

Her eyes lifted to his. 'And what was it for you?'

'He wasn't entirely wrong. The wolf represents what family should be about, the pack instinct. Loyalty, communication, protection, shared wisdom…everything my father isn't.'

'Oh…' no bliss now, just sadness '…hence the rebellion?'

He nodded, holding her gaze—the sense that she got him, that they got each other overwhelming, overpowering even. A connection that ran far deeper than such a brief encounter would ordinarily permit.

And then she smiled, her lashes lowering, one hand lifting to his neck.

'What about this one…?' She touched her fingers to his clavicle, the pads soft and tantalising as she stroked them lower.

'That's the tip of a wedge-tailed eagle in flight.'

'An eagle?' Her eyes didn't leave his chest. 'How big is it?'

He took hold of her hand. 'It goes from here…' he traced her finger along his collarbone '…to here…' around his shoulder '…and all the way along the back, to right about…here.'

With her hand now hooked over his shoulder, he leaned closer, his gaze falling to her softly parted lips. 'He represents strength, courage, and freedom.'

'Freedom from your father?'

Yes, she got him, all right.

'Are there more?'

'More?' He was struggling to focus. This close he could see the inner ring of fire around her pupils, could see the light dusting of freckles beneath her make-up, along her cheeks and the bridge of her nose, all the more prominent with the lustful flush to her skin. And her lips, hell, she kept wetting them, leaving a glossy trail that was driving him crazy.

He tried to breathe but all he got was her scent… sun and sex, tangled up in the beer they had drunk. A surprising and enticing aphrodisiac.

'More animals,' she said, 'more ink?'

Right, they were still on the tattoos…

'Yes.'

'I'd like to see.'

'You would?'

This wasn't the norm. He didn't just meet a girl, share a few drinks and… He swallowed the sudden tightness in his chest. A sudden burst of nerves that he didn't understand.

She nodded. 'If you'd like to show me…?'

'Are you sure?'

She blinked, the fire in her eyes dimming. 'Not if you're not.' She started to turn away. 'I'm sorry, this really isn't like me. I don't know what I was thinking—'

'I think you were thinking exactly what I was thinking.'

She gave a choked laugh. 'You don't know what you're saying.'

'Don't I?' He took her hand, angled her back towards him, waiting for those blue eyes to reach his before assuring her, 'I don't do this either. But this connection between us is something else and if you're sure you want to explore it, I will take you to my room right now. *Every* tattoo yours to read.'

She pressed her lips together, her nostrils flaring with her breath, her eyes alight once more. 'I'd like that.'

CHAPTER THREE

EVE HUFFED OUT a breath and tucked her head beneath the pillow, hiding from the dawning light threatening to penetrate her eyelids before she was ready.

What had she been thinking?

Thinking? Her self-conscious laughed. *There had been* no *thinking.*

She'd been too busy losing herself in the company of a man who made her feel more than she had in years, revelling in his attention, his flirtation, his genuine interest in everything about her.

Not her skills as a PR specialist, not her standing in society, not her sisterly wisdom as the emotionally detached outsider of the family.

Just her. Eve.

And it had been thrilling and intoxicating and everything she'd needed from the moment she'd stepped off the plane onto Australian soil.

And now she was in his bed. Not her hotel room. His.

And though she hated to admit it, reality beckoned, aka Garrison Downs and her sisters, and it was time to move. But first…she wasn't so crass as to kiss and run.

Though 'kiss' was an understatement of epic proportions.

A night of wild, intense lovemaking with a sprinkling of therapy more like. A connection that she hadn't been looking for, hadn't needed, but it had found her anyway.

The kind of connection life had taught her to run from—not indulge in. Because intense passion was for fools. It didn't last. It didn't equate to the perfect life, happy wife. Life lesson learned, courtesy of Ma and Pa.

So exit stage left…if she could just find it…or him.

Because now she thought on it, she couldn't hear him. She wasn't aware of him close by. No heavy breathing. No movement. Just the gentle hum of the air-conditioning unit.

Reaching out, she tentatively probed the sheets. Cold. Vacant. She peeled open one eye, wincing against the light leaking through the pale curtains.

White walls, wooden floor, a bedside table, wardrobe, her carelessly tossed clothing on a chair and two doors. One to the bathroom, one to the outdoors.

But no man.

Had he left before she could? Something deep within her squirmed and it wasn't the relief her head told her to feel.

She groaned and hid back under the pillow. Night one of her homecoming and she'd already lost her head. It didn't bode well for the rest of her trip, didn't bode well at—

The door clicked open then closed. Her pulse tripped out, rapping as loud as his boots against the floor. She peered out from beneath her fluff-filled haven and...*oh my*, he was even better looking the morning after.

'Hey...' She scraped her hair out of her face, tried to moisten her mouth that felt as dry as sandpaper.

'Morning, gorgeous.'

Gorgeous? Hardly!

'Took a punt you were a coffee drinker.'

He lifted his hands. Two takeaway cups, paper bags too—he'd been out fetching her breakfast! Her heart gave another wild beat and she pushed herself up, tugging the sheet with her.

'I can't believe you brought me coffee.'

'I did, but if you'd rather something else I can nip back out.'

'No. Coffee's perfect.' She tried for a smile. 'Thank you.'

Coffee was more than perfect. He was more than perfect. How did he look so good so early? Smell so good too. All fresh and masculine. Citrus and oak. He must have showered while she'd slept and the idea of him naked in the next room, under the jets, was enough to slice through the morning fog and have a heat coiling down low.

He passed her a cup. 'You're sure?'

'Absolutely.' She strengthened her smile, lifted

the lid off the coffee and breathed in the aroma with a sigh. 'Caffeine. The nectar of the gods.'

'You'll hear no argument from me.' He settled back beside her. The scene too cosy by far. She peeked his way. Watched as he took a sip of his own, marvelled at his profile in the fresh light of day and decided. He was the best-looking man she had ever met. And last night… Her cheeks and belly warmed. Scenes flashing before her mind.

'About last night…' She wet her lips. 'I'm sorry if I was… I hope I wasn't…too much.'

His mouth twitched, his eyes flashed. 'Define what you mean by too much.'

She swallowed her rising blush. 'I know I can be quite forceful.'

'You were that.'

'And demanding.'

'You were that too.'

'And I like to take control.'

'You definitely do.'

There was no swallowing *this* blush. But he was grinning, the heat in his eyes nursing the salacious ache low in her abdomen.

And then she remembered how she must look, how she must…*smell*.

'You okay?'

'Yeah.' *No.*

'You're doing that nose thing…'

'I'm fine.' She forced her nose to behave, tried to smooth back her morning bush of a hairdo and sipped at her coffee, praying it would reinstate her sense of calm.

'I'll pretend I believe you.'

His response tickled her, provoking a smile she wouldn't have thought possible.

'Breakfast?' He offered her one of the bags. 'Now, in the interests of full disclosure, I figured you were an avocado on sourdough kind of a girl, but this is what you really need.'

She eyed him, eyed the bag that already had signs of grease seeping through, and her nose wrinkled further. 'Which is?'

'One of Jenna's infamous brekky burgers.'

'Jenna of Roarke's Cafe?'

'You know it?'

She looked inside the bag. Greasy and very much *not* her thing. 'I didn't think Jenna would still be there.'

'So long as Jenna walks the earth, she'll be there.'

She smiled, the bittersweet memory of Mum taking her and her sisters there after school for the occasional treat coming back to her. The stacked pancakes, lashings of syrup and bacon. Even a dollop of cream too.

'Now, that smile's more like it.'

The approval in his tone caught at her chest. Coupled with his kindness and compassion, he was teasing at a part of her she kept locked away. A part she *needed* to keep locked away.

'Ever tried one?'

'Huh?'

'A brekky burger?' He gave her a bemused smile. 'It's not as bad as it looks, I promise.'

Grateful he'd misread her reaction, she placed her coffee down and rolled back the paper. 'If you say so.'

'You'll thank me for it later.' He took a bite of his own with an unrestrained groan. 'And they're as good as ever.'

Unconvinced, she gave it a tentative sniff. 'And what's in it? Exactly.'

'Best just try it first… Dare you.'

A laugh bubbled up. 'You *dare* me?'

'Uh-huh.'

She shook her head, her smile growing. What was it about this guy? Knowing just what to say to make her smile, laugh, to do just as he asked…

She scooped out the overstuffed bread roll, met his gaze and took a hefty bite and… *Oh, my!*

She chewed as her taste buds sang, confused but elated. So much going on, so much deliciousness and naughtiness and all in one mouthful. Bacon. Egg. Cheese. Potato. Onion. And…oh, that sauce!

She took another bite, and closed her eyes on a blissful sigh. She felt better already. Okay, so it seemed coffee, a brekky burger, and Nate were the perfect wake-up call. She opened her eyes to admit he was right and found him watching her, the heat in his gaze working with the heat still simmering within her.

'Jenna should get you to advertise, she'd make millions if not billions.'

'I really don't think any company would want me as their frontman right now.'

'How can you say that?'

'Because I haven't bathed, haven't done my make-up and my hair looks like I've been zapped by lightning. I'm hardly the vision of health.'

'You couldn't be more wrong.' It was gruff, sincere, the intensity of his gaze stealing her breath away. 'Your cheeks are glowing, your eyes are bright, your hair is wild for sure, but it suits you. And it's taking my all not to throw breakfast aside and devour you instead.'

'You need glasses…' but it came out breathless, heated, the riot of butterflies within her impossible to ignore.

'There's nothing wrong with my sight.'

'You sure about that?'

'Never more.'

She swallowed the wedge in her throat, wet her lips and he tracked the move, hungry but not for food. 'Your burger will get cold.'

'A price I'm willing to pay.'

'Nate, I…'

You what? You want him to stop saying all the sweet things? You want him to stop making you feel *all the sweet things? Just get out of bed, get dressed and take your breakfast with you. Thank him for a great night and leave it at that.*

It was the sensible thing to do.

The right thing to do.

Only her body wasn't obeying.

He was leaning closer, the sheet covering her modesty slowly slipping away, caressing her sensitised skin…

'Nate,' she breathed.

'Eve,' he breathed back.

They came together, fierce and desperate. Breakfast shoved aside for their lips, their bodies…

She tugged his T-shirt up and over his head as he joined her beneath the sheets, his fingers biting into her behind as she hooked her leg around him, moaning as the hard ridge of his jeans came up against the sensitised heart of her.

She arched back as he deepened their kiss, heat rushing through her middle, filling her breasts as her nipples hardened against the tantalising wall of his chest. The rough friction of his body driving her to the precipice.

He pressed his forehead to hers, sucked in a breath. 'How can you not see what a temptress you are?'

She laughed, the sound tight in her chest, her throat, his words too much like something out of a romance novel. Books she had once loved and devoured, then dismissed as fantastical nonsense the day she'd learnt the truth about her parents.

About the fickleness of love.

'Anyone ever tell you you talk too much?' she murmured, beating back the chill trying to work its way in as she pushed him onto his back and fenced him in with her thighs.

He gave a throaty chuckle. 'And there she is, the lioness coming out to play.'

She nipped his lip. 'Are you complaining?'

'Not for a second.'

She held his fiery gaze as she undid his jeans. 'Good, because I don't need you whispering sweet nothings, Nate.'

'Even when they're not nothing?'

'Ooh, a double negative,' she teased, though her throat contracted, her heart too.

'I'll give you a double…'

He palmed her neck and brought her swiftly down to meet his kiss. Hard and unrelenting. As though he sensed her need to block out all else but this.

They kissed until her panic subsided and need took over. Kissed until it was him on top of her and he finished the job she'd started, shucking the rest of his clothing. He reached into his jeans for his wallet and protection, sheathed himself in a heartbeat and then he was rising over her. His mouth feverish against hers, his hands stroking and teasing and making her plead.

'Please, Nate, I want you.'

He nudged her thighs around him. 'I want you too.'

He pushed inside her with a groan that had her body trembling and tightening in one. He pressed a kiss to her ear, defiantly whispered sweet nothings—delicious things about the way she felt, the things he wanted to do, all things that her body revelled in and she was helpless to deny. Driving her higher as she rocked with him, savouring it all.

Life forgotten in a moment of bliss that had her crying out his name, over and over.

She clung to the high, wanting to keep it, extend it, rejoice in it for ever...

Though for ever was an impossibility. She knew it even as she fought for it. And as he cried out her name, she reciprocated, her muscles contracting as pleasure took over, shattering within her, a thousand tiny eruptions making her shudder and shake.

She rode the wave with him, moved with him, breathed with him. Perfect unison.

Until he sank down beside her, his arm heavy across her middle, kissed her shoulder and held her close. Held her as though she were his to hold. And she stared at the ceiling. Stared so hard she could blame the dampness in her eyes on her failure to blink because, hell, she wanted to cry. Again.

And why?

It was silly. Stupid. They'd had a great night. A great morning.

She should be happy, elated. Ready to leave on a high.

'Coffee, a brekky burger and sex for breakfast,' Nate murmured, his breath hot on her neck. 'I'd say we're the vision of domestic bliss, wouldn't you?'

Hell, no. Because domestic bliss suggested something more. Something serious. Something with the impossible: longevity.

'I should go.'

His body pulled taut, his head lifting. 'Now?'

'Yes.'

He was trying to catch her eye, but she was inching away, slipping free of his grasp.

'But you haven't finished your breakfast.'

'I'll take it with me.'

She was already on her feet, gathering up her clothes and her suitcase as she hurried into the bathroom. She closed the door and fought the urge to sink against it, refusing to succumb to her racing thoughts as she focused on what she had to do, as a robot would a routine. Freshened up. Tied her hair back. Forwent the usual make-up. Threw on the first clothes that came to hand—silk cami and floaty pants—and donned her ballet pumps for a quick exit.

She needed to get out of there.

When she emerged, he was clothed and sitting up against the headboard, one leg crossed over the other. Everything about him relaxed save for his eyes as they met her own.

'Better?'

She cleared her throat, gripped the handle of her suitcase as though it were the only thing holding her up. And it probably was. Her body still weak with the echo of her orgasm, the rebellious desire to lose her head and slip back beneath the sheets, too.

'Much. Thank you for breakfast…and for last night.'

'No need to thank me.' His voice was rich, thick with whatever thoughts he'd been entertaining in her absence. 'I think we both got something out of it.'

'We did.'

She headed for the door, kept her focus on it and the sensible decision to be free of whatever this was between them.

'You really are going, then?'

She missed her footing. Thank heaven she was wearing flats. 'I think that's for the best.'

'Can I see you again?'

She swallowed. Didn't turn. 'I don't think that's a good idea.'

She heard his feet hit the floor, the bed groan as he stood. 'Correct me if I'm wrong but everything we've shared so far has felt pretty good.'

'It has,' she conceded, her voice husky with the lustful remnants of the night, the morning, the way he made her feel, not just with his body, but his gentle words too. He paused behind her, his proximity warm against her skin, and she made herself turn and face him. 'Let's not ruin it by trying to make it into something more.'

'Who says it'll ruin it?'

'I do. I'm only in town for a few months and then I'm getting out of here. And I don't intend to look back.'

Not on you, or this place, her head added for emphasis, trying to drown out her heart, which wanted more, so much more.

'Months in which we can have more fun and get to know one another.'

Months in which he could learn that there was nothing more worth loving beneath the surface. Months in which she would be forced to watch the fire in his eyes die out and his interest wane. Months when she should be concentrating on the mess she and her sisters were in, and not the messed-up state her parents' marriage had left her in.

'Nate, there's no future here. I have no interest in getting serious, not now, not ever.'

'That's quite the statement.'

His brows drew together, a lock of hair teasing over one and making her fingers itch to stroke it back. She curled them into her palm.

'What it is, is the truth. I told you, work is my life. I don't have time for a relationship. I don't want a relationship.'

His mouth tugged to one side as he cocked his head, his gaze intense, searching... What was he looking for? A sign that she was lying? A chance to change her mind?

'I have to go,' she whispered.

'Scared you'll change your mind?'

'No. I formed this opinion long ago and one night isn't going to change it. No matter how much fun we had.'

'Fun we were still having up until twenty minutes ago.'

And don't think on it, Eve, not right now.

She turned away before he could lure her in.

'I'm not asking you to marry me, Eve, I'm asking you to date me.'

Now she laughed, his choice of words as amusing as they were triggering. If only he knew the real reason she was here, the 'M' clause, what would he say then?

'Eve?' Gently he turned her to face him. The look in his sexy come-to-bed eyes made her heart sigh. Would it be so bad? A little bit of fun to offset the misery of returning home.

Fun that had the capacity to turn into something else. Something more. Something dangerous. She only had to think on her parents to know that giving such passion any real airtime was asking for a lifetime of regret. Only…

She pressed her lips together, her eyes falling to his. One last kiss in exchange for a lifetime of denial couldn't hurt, could it? She reached up, breathed in his scent, pressed a palm to his warm chest and swept her lips against his, savouring every bit of it, of him.

Then…

He blinked down at her as she fell back, a thousand unspoken questions in his depths and, for one senseless second, she yearned for him to tug her back. Then she remembered her mother's pain, her father's guilt, and her grandmother's cautioning words, 'If you lose your head to your heart, what can you expect?'

Heartache. That was what.

'Goodbye, Nate.'

CHAPTER FOUR

THIS WASN'T HOW Eve had planned her return to Garrison Downs to go.

She'd planned to use the taxi ride to clear her head, her emotions…to see to it that she strode in as the woman she was now. Always composed. Always in control. And determined to get the answers she needed to put an end to this insanity.

Instead, her head was as messed up as her heart.

And she missed London. She missed the hustle and the bustle and the ability to think straight in a sea of people she didn't know.

They'd been driving for almost an hour, red dirt and blue sky for as far as the eye could see. The only verdant relief coming from the sporadic pockets of mallee scrub and saltbush, not a building or a human in sight.

So very isolating and…*ha*, she wanted to say cold, but the chill only existed within her. Courtesy of the past rather than her surroundings. And the closer they got to her childhood home, the more her gut shifted from brekky-burger splendour to roller-coaster turmoil. Because she couldn't be here without feeling it, every memory trying to work its way to the surface. The good, the bad...the ugly.

There was a part of her—a worryingly large part—that wanted to race back to Nate's hotel room and seek out the oblivion he effortlessly provided. Because by his side she hadn't cared about any of this.

No, that wasn't quite true. She'd *cared*, but she'd felt invincible, untouchable, able to deal with anything and everything because he'd been there. Helping her rise above it.

'Here, miss?'

The taxi driver sent her a look over his shoulder and she nodded, her gaze drifting to the gates looming tall on the horizon. The wooden arch with its giant bull horns and the name Garrison Downs burnt deep into the vertical posts. Posts that bore another man's name...a man who now had a chance to take it all back.

She cursed. 'Over my dead body.'

'What was that?' The taxi driver caught her eye in the rear-view mirror and she nipped her lip.

'Nothing. Just thinking aloud...'

Only it wasn't 'nothing', it was everything. For Rose at least. And she had to see the future secure for them all, her sisters, her family...even if that word had lost some of its meaning over the years.

The car slowed as they rolled through the gates, the noise within changing as the road smoothed, the winding driveway almost as long as the town of Marni itself, though the house ahead was more

Parisian paradise than Outback grandeur. The luscious gardens surrounding it, too.

An architectural masterpiece, two years in the making and built when Eve had been a child. Dad's project. For Mum. He'd wanted to create the ultimate home from home, a home that was hers rather than the one they'd shared with his parents. Both long gone now but, back then, Grandma's austere and judgemental presence had been enough to make anyone want their own space. Pop included. And though the old homestead still existed, it was tucked off to the left and hidden by the countless trees Dad had seen planted—the perfect finishing touch to what had been a romantic gesture of gargantuan proportions.

Or so her father claimed.

Now Eve thought about it, Ana's age meant it had to have been built around the time she was born. And didn't that make it the ultimate act of guilt, rather than a gift born of love and thought, care and devotion?

Her stomach rolled anew, and she tugged her gaze from the incriminating structure to take in the distant hills to the east. Hills that housed steep ravines and shady canyons. Dams fed by the many water sources Garrison Downs was blessed enough to have access and the rights to use. Hectares of land for the station's cattle to graze.

She imagined Rose out there now, working hard with her jillaroos and jackaroos. September was their second muster season, she'd be busy from sun-up till sundown, likely too busy to see Eve until she rolled home that night.

Too late and too exhausted to talk…one could hope.

The car came to a stop and Eve lowered her sunglasses.

You've got this.

Pulling her handbag over her shoulder, she reached for the door handle just as movement from the nearest paddock caught her eye. A bay horse and its rider were galloping towards her, a dog hot on their tail.

Rose. She didn't need to see a defining feature to know it in her blood. She took a breath…*here goes*…and pushed open the door.

At least Rose wanted to welcome her back…that was a good sign at least…or not.

Rose drew to a halt at the edge of the field, dismounted and secured her horse's reins to the fence before turning to face Eve. Eve whose heart was in her throat as she stood, ballet pumps rooted to the hard-packed dirt, head racing with how this would play out.

Did she hug, kiss, stand back…shake a hand even?

The derisive slant to Rose's mouth didn't help, not when it was all she could see of her sister's face beneath the rim of her hat as she strode towards her. The dog in step beside her.

'I'll be off then, miss,' the cabbie said, depositing her luggage at her feet.

She thanked him and he sped off, likely keen to

get back to civilisation and she fought the urge to run after him, her attention back on Rose. *Forbidding*, Rose.

In this moment, they appeared as different as night and day.

Rose in her well-worn boots, equally worn Akubra, functional brown ponytail, dust-covered jeans and long-sleeved shirt. All designed to protect as much of her from the sun as possible. While Eve had no such concern.

Her cami was too skimpy, her floaty pants too thin, and she hadn't donned a hat of any kind in so long...unless it was ladies' day at the races, for which she'd wear the most elaborate hair accessory. All for show. None of it practical.

'You remembered where we live, then?' Rose paused a few strides away, her familiar lilt making Eve's heart warm even as she held herself back. The invisible gulf between them ever more pronounced now that they were face to face, her sister's taunt making clear she wasn't ready to cross it.

But then, neither was Eve.

She cocked her head. 'Morning to you too, sis.'

Rose pressed her lips together, her eyes drifting to the luggage at her feet.

'I thought you were staying for a few months...?'

'I am.' Eve lifted her chin. 'I can travel light, you know.'

Travel light and with clothes that wouldn't last two seconds in this part of the world...*nice one, Eve!*

A blatant sign that her brain had quit firing as it should days, if not weeks, ago.

Rose's eyes returned to Eve's, her Waverly blue depths flashing with something…defiance, anger, hurt…but Eve was too caught up in the realisation that they all had those eyes. Dad's eyes. Ana, too. And it was a punch to the gut.

'Well, come on, then,' Rose blustered, flicking the dust out of her ponytail and waving at the house. 'You want a hand with that?' She gave a clipped nod at the case.

'No.' Did her sister really think her *that* incapable? 'I can do it myself.'

Just as she had with all the other, metaphorical baggage she'd carried around all these years…

She threw her travel bag over her shoulder and yanked the case into motion, grateful that it behaved this time, and followed her sister to the house, grimacing as her ballet pumps collected red dust like static on a balloon.

'Thinking about leaving already?'

She looked up to find Rose staring at her from the deck of the porch, her eyes bright with the accusation. Her dog made its own noise too as it sank down next to a bowl filled with water.

'Good girl, Blossom,' her sister murmured, without looking. And Eve realised it was staying put. As a working dog, she wouldn't be allowed inside the house. A rule their mother had laid down…

Hats off, boots off, leave the work at the door!

Save for Father's study, of course. That was his domain. His rules.

And, of course, Rose would be the same.

'Eve?'

'Of course not,' she said, dragging herself out of the memories and up the steps.

But it was no use. As she crossed the threshold, the past assaulted her from every direction. The family heirlooms from their father's side, the exquisite furnishings carefully chosen by their mother, paintings and artefacts inspired by Mum's love of travel…travel that she'd rarely got to enjoy after her marriage because Dad had been married to the land first.

And it didn't matter that it was a vast open space, light and tranquil. High ceilings, white walls, dark-wood accents and polished parquet floor. She might as well have been buried six feet under for all she was suffocated by it.

'You look like you've seen a ghost…'

Barely aware of Rose's remark, Eve gave the smallest shake of her head.

'Why don't you leave your bags there?' Rose tossed her hat and boots into the mudroom and Eve followed suit with her pumps. 'I've had Lindy arrange us breakfast out by the pool.'

'It's okay, I've already…'

Rose sent her a look that had her refusal dying on her tongue, the uncertain teen she'd once been creeping to the surface…

But you're not that teen any more. You're a suc-

cessful businesswoman with your own mind, your own will.

'I've already eaten,' she said, releasing her suitcase and dumping her travel bag on top.

'I haven't.'

Eve's mouth twisted to the side. Her sister's message clear. You're coming with me, whether you're eating or not.

And looking at the shadows beneath Rose's eyes, the worry creasing up her brow, Eve realised she owed her big sister this. A conversation that was long overdue.

'Okay,' she acquiesced. 'Breakfast it is.'

They walked through the house, Eve's gaze fixed on her sister and not the memory prompts clamouring for attention. Finally able to breathe when they entered the colonial-inspired pool room with its many French doors thrown open to the gardens beyond. It was a secluded oasis, a place where one could readily forget where they were in the world... where *she* was.

'Thank you, Lindy,' Rose said as a dark-haired woman, buxom and petite, hurried in with a heavily laden tray. 'Eve, this is our housekeeper, Lindy.' Rose pulled out a chair at the table and sat. 'Lindy, meet Eve, my sister.'

Lindy gave Eve a shy smile, her cheeks flushing as she set the tray down with barely a clatter. 'It's a pleasure to meet you.'

'And you,' Eve said, taking a seat beside her sister as Lindy laid out all the items. Water, coffee, juice, toast, fruit, eggs, meats…

Rose surveyed the outdoors as Eve surveyed her. The shadows beneath her sister's eyes were ever more prominent in the bright light of the room, the lines of worry in her face, too…but it was the hollowness to her cheeks that concerned Eve most. Was her sister not eating properly? Was it the exhaustion? The grief? The threat to the station?

'You knew, didn't you?' Rose said quietly, after Lindy had left. 'All this time you knew about Dad's affair and you said nothing.'

'What *could* I say?' Eve said, just as soft. 'You were Dad's shadow, you idolised him.'

'So?' Rose came alive, her head flicking around, her ponytail with it. 'You shouldn't have shouldered that on your own, Evie. I'm your sister! Your *big* sister. It was my responsibility to bear that burden, not yours!'

Eve choked on a laugh. 'You think being the oldest means you deserve that burden?'

'No one deserves that kind of burden…but you could've shared it.'

'I shared it with Mum. I shared it with Dad. And believe me, that only made it worse.'

Rose's eyes blazed. 'They both knew that you knew?'

'About the affair, yes. But I didn't know about Ana. I don't think even Mum knew about her…'

Rose took an unsteady breath, shook her head.

'It's why Dad let me go to England without a fight.'

'He was scared you'd tell us?'

'No, I think he knew his sordid secret was safe with me. It was bad enough to have my own illusion shattered. The idea of you and Tilly suffering the same… I couldn't do it. And Mum didn't want me to. She'd already gone through enough.'

'So why let you go?'

Eve gave a twisted smile. 'I don't think he could bear the look in my eye, it wasn't love that he saw any more, but judgement, hatred even.'

'And did you? *Hate* him?'

No words would come. No rebuttal. No affirmation. Eve… Eve couldn't answer.

Instead, she leaned forward and poured them both some iced water. Took a sip of her own, wishing it could get rid of the bitter taste in her throat.

But only an end to this conversation had that power.

'How did you find out?'

Eve's breath shuddered through her, the ice rattling in her glass as she placed it down before she dropped it. Now she wished she'd said something—*anything* to stop her sister asking that!

'I'm sorry, Evie, I don't want to cause you any more pain but—'

'I was fifteen,' she said over her, forcing the words through clenched teeth, knowing she had to get it over with and hating it all the same. 'It was the night of the Marni Cup ball…'

An event that was considered the highlight of the year at Garrison Downs. People travelled from all over to attend the two-day racing carnival hosted by her parents. Everyone who was anyone in attendance. It took weeks to prepare for and was the talk of the social elite long after it was over. But for Eve, that night had been memorable for all the wrong reasons.

'I was smitten with the new station hand Dad had employed. Rip, remember him?'

Rose frowned. 'Cook's cousin's kid? He was a right 'un...'

Eve gave a gruff laugh. 'He was a little rough round the edges, I admit, but I had this fantastical notion that I could change him.'

'Just like all those books you loved to read.'

'Just like all those books...' Eve echoed. 'I was so busy mooning over him as he played valet outside that I was barely aware of the ball and the company within. I'd managed to lose myself in the curtain when Mum passed by, Clay Garrison hot on her tail.'

'Clay? I swear that man's name is cropping up far too often these days.'

'Yeah, well, he was talking to her, his voice too low to hear but I could tell Mum was trying to get away. She was pale and jittery. And the more Clay smiled, the more Mum wilted. I forgot all about Rip and became Mum's shadow after that. She wasn't the same. She was polite with everyone, you know Mum, for ever the hostess, but she was distant. She wasn't so quick with the smiles, or the conversation, and I was worried. I thought about asking her outright, but I didn't want to make it worse, so after the party was over, I went to Dad's study. I wanted to tell him something was wrong. He was Mum's greatest protector, right? I trusted him to get to the bottom of it and fix it. But Mum was already there. They were arguing.'

'Oh, Evie…' Rose pressed a hand to her chest, clearly sensing where this was heading, and Eve nodded, swallowing down the sickness rising with the memory.

'Clay had seen Dad with someone in Melbourne, claimed they looked *close*.'

'Why, that piece of…'

'Dad swore it wasn't how it looked. Swore he'd ended things with Lili years ago. Lili! Like, who the hell was Lili? And what did he mean, *ended* it?'

Eve shook her head, remembering the moment she'd heard her own father confirm the unthinkable. Her father. Her hero. The man she had so desperately wanted to please, to be seen by…to finally step out of Rose's shadow and be noticed by…had been no better than a scoundrel, a cheat…unworthy of her love, or any love for that matter.

'I was so angry, Rose. I stormed in, tore a strip off him and he…' Eve choked on unshed tears '…he cowered. I'd never seen Dad cower, but he did. He sank behind that massive desk of his, head in his hands, and I carried on, consumed by this…this *anger*.' She fisted her chest, the visceral strength of it vibrating through her. 'Mum tried to calm me down, pleaded with me to stop, that I didn't understand… I mean, what was there to understand? He'd had an affair, betrayed her, betrayed us all. I couldn't bear it. There he was hiding behind his desk and Mum was *defending* him! *Actually* defending him! Telling me it wasn't as simple as all of that…that one day I'd understand. Like somehow, I was too young to get it.'

'You were fifteen…' Rose whispered.

'Plenty old enough to understand what Dad had done.'

'But not the reason.'

Eve's frown was sharp. 'Don't *you* start defending him!'

'I'm not. I'm…' Rose took a breath. 'I'm angry that he kept Ana from us. I'm angry that any of it had to happen at all…'

'Why do I feel like there's a but coming, Rose?'

Her sister was quiet for a long moment. Too long.

'Rose!'

'You should read Mum's journal,' her sister said, soft but sure.

'The one that Matilda found in Dad's study?'

She nodded.

'I don't want to read it.'

'It will help you to understand.'

'By reliving Mum's pain, no, thank you.'

'Dad was hurting too.'

Eve snorted, pulling her knees up to her chest and

hugging them tight. A defensive move she hadn't needed in so long.

'They both played their part in the breakdown of their marriage, Evie, but they came back from it. Stronger and more in love than ever. You'd know that if you read the journal.'

'They lied to us, Rose, they lied to the world. Playing at happy families. What a joke.'

'It wasn't a joke, it was real. Their love for each other and us.'

'How can you say that after Ana?'

Rose picked at some invisible speck on her thigh. 'Because I remember before, I remember when things weren't right, and I'd catch them arguing…'

This was news to Eve but then Rose was older, she would have seen more, been more aware.

'…times when things weren't so good, and Mum would withdraw. She'd sit in that chair in Dad's study and lose herself in the view.'

'I used to think she did that because she longed for him to come back,' Eve said, remembering the same. 'Now I think she did it because she longed for home. For England. For her life from before. Like a prisoner looking out from her cell.'

Rose's wounded blue eyes flicked to her. 'That's a bit extreme.'

'Is it?' Eve blurted back. 'You just told me it's where she would retreat to.'

'When times were bad, yes. Not helped by her parents cutting her off like they did—'

'They were hurt, Rose. Devastated when she left.'

'And I'm in no mood to argue about *them* right now.'

And neither was Eve. The time to try and heal her sister's relationship with Granny Lavigne come…she just had to stick around long enough.

'Yes, Mum may have missed home, but she was happy, Evie. She got better, and she was happy— she *was*,' Rose stressed as Eve arched her brows. 'And she took to that chair and counted down the seconds until Dad returned from the paddocks. She also sat there, longing for our return too. From school, from days out without her. She'd sit there and wait for you and Tilly to come back from boarding school in the holidays, heartbroken when you stopped coming.'

'Don't twist this onto me.'

'I'm not. I'm trying to make you see that there's more than one side to a story and until you take them all into account you won't see the full picture.'

Rose watched her, waiting for her to accept it rather than reject it. And Eve stared at the pool, mocking her sister's patience because as much as Eve's heart wanted to listen, her head was saying no. It would be a cold day in hell before Eve picked up that journal.

'At least go and see Ana. She's our sister, Evie.'

'*Half*-sister,' she corrected, heart fluttering inside her chest.

'Still our sister, and, from all I can gather, her

mother did right by ours. Lili loved Dad, too. And
she didn't want to tear our family apart. There's
something to admire and respect in that. She isn't
the enemy, and neither is Ana…and neither is Dad.
He wasn't perfect, no man is, but he loved us. He
loved *you*.'

Eve said nothing because she couldn't. Inside,
her heart was shattering into a thousand tiny pieces
and she didn't know how to piece it back together.
It was *too late* to piece it back together.

'Please, Evie, you need to find closure before it
ruins you and your life.'

'Me and my life are doing pretty darn well, thank
you.'

'So, you think it's okay that you fled from your
home, from us, and you've carried on fleeing.'

'I'm hardly fleeing, Rose,' she threw back at her.
'I'm here now, aren't I?'

'You didn't come to Tilly's wedding.'

'I was tying up loose ends at work so I could be
here now.'

Rose raised both brows.

'Okay. Okay, so I didn't want to come and put a
damper on the whole affair.'

'You should have been there. If you'd only seen
for yourself how happy they are.'

'I know they're happy, Rose, I don't doubt it. But
for how long?'

'I'm not saying they won't face their challenges,
everyone does, but so long as they have their love,
they'll get through it.'

'Just like Mum and Dad…'

'*Yes.*'

Eve was being sarcastic. Rose wasn't. And after a long delay where her sister was probably hoping for some miraculous change on Eve's part, Rose sighed.

'I wish you'd said something. All these years, I could've been there for you, we could've faced it together.'

'What difference would it have made?'

'It could've made all the difference. We could've confronted them together. Mum might have opened up. She might have told us about her postnatal depression. Given us both the chance to understand and for you to make amends before…'

Rose swallowed, blinked away the tears that threatened and Eve did the same, silently finishing her sister's sentence for her…*before it was too late.*

Before they'd lost them both and Eve had lost all those years too.

'What ifs don't help anyone, Rose.' Eve had realised that a long time ago. 'And learning about Mum's depression from her journal…' she shuddered '…and the doctor's notes Tilly found. It just feels wrong.'

'I don't know. I think if you read them, you'd feel differently. It feels like Mum wanted us to—'

'Leave it, Rose. *Please.*'

Her sister dragged in a breath, her blue eyes swirling with sorrow, and it pained Eve that she'd put that look there. No, not entirely her, it was their father too.

And it was his legacy that had them stewing in this crisis now.

'You know what gets me,' Eve said, clinging to the anger. 'That Dad did nothing. That a man who couldn't even stand by his own vows, was happy to see us forced into giving our own.'

Rose huffed. 'I'm not sure he knew about the condition.'

'Oh, he knew, Rose. Dad knew everything there was to know about this place. He wouldn't have missed that clause.'

'You think?'

'You don't?'

Rose considered it a while then, 'If that were the case, why didn't he do something about it?'

'Damned if I know, but I'm going to get us out of it.'

Rose gave a weak smile. 'I appreciate your optimism but, until we have a plan, I fail to share it.'

'Look, I know we said we'd keep it a secret, the condition, Ana's existence…but maybe it's time we went to the press with it all, or at least consider leaking it.'

'Hell, no!'

'Think about it, Rose, they'd have a field day. The very idea that an inheritance would be denied because we're the—' Eve made air quotes '—*weaker* sex? Can you imagine?'

'I am imagining, and it would be hell.'

'Worse than marriage to some guy we barely know, because I'm not seeing anyone and I'm pretty sure you're not.'

Nate flashed before her mind's eye and she promptly put him back in the box.

'Yes, worse! They'd be camped out on the doorstep. Ana and her family wouldn't be able to breathe for the speculation, the gossip, the cameras and the interrogation. And then there's that cad, Clay, he'd be straight on us trying to make sure we don't comply just to see the land return to him and that can't happen, Evie.'

Their gazes drifted to the garden, to the land that they could lose, the air weighing heavy in their silence as the wind rustled through the trees.

'I'll pay Harrington a visit first thing Monday,' Eve said eventually. 'Apply some pressure, see what's what.'

'Okay.' Rose nodded. 'That sounds like a plan. You can take the truck, but tread carefully, won't you? I don't think George is all that well.'

Eve's ears pricked up. 'Really?'

'The last few times I've seen him, he's not been right.'

'In what sense? Poorly or…?'

'Yes, poorly, what else did you think I meant?'

'I was wondering whether his ability to do his job had come into question.'

'I don't think there's any suggestion of that.'

'I'll suggest it if it means we can find a way out of this mess.'

'Play nice, Evie.'

'He's a man, I don't need to play nice.'

'Not all men are bad.'

'Not all men are good either.'

And just like that they were back to Dad.

'The affair was a moment, a blip. They chose to move on from it together and they made it work. They *loved* one another.'

Eve said nothing, answer enough, and Rose blew out a breath. 'Right, I should get back.'

'You don't need to tell me twice,' Eve murmured, looking up as her sister stood. 'It's muster season, it's all hands on paddock.'

Their father had said it so many times over, Eve could hear him now.

'It's good to know you still have the Outback in you somewhere.'

And Dad, her sister meant, and Eve shook her head with a choked laugh. 'Buried *very* deep. Now go, get yourself out of here, before Aaron has to come find you.'

Rose grimaced. 'Don't even joke about it.'

'Problems in paradise?' Aaron was her second in command…could there be tensions between them now Dad was gone?

'Nothing I can't handle.'

Eve didn't doubt it. Rose would handle it as she handled *everything* in life. With care and stoic determination. She hadn't run at the first sign of adversity. She'd stuck it out. Built her life around it.

Unlike Eve, who, as Rose had rightly pointed out, ran.

Just as she'd run from Nate that morning. Nate and his sweet breakfast offering and sexy grin. Her heart gave a squeeze.

'Make sure you take some food with you,' she said, doing her best to ignore it and focus on her sister. Her sister and her worryingly slender finger. 'You have a long day ahead.'

Rose scrunched up her face as she redid her ponytail. 'I may have bent the truth when I said I hadn't eaten…'

'Oh, right, sneaky.'

'I had to get you to talk to me.'

'I know,' Eve said softly, 'and it feels good to have talked.'

'It does.'

They shared a smile, so much passing between them as they blinked away fresh tears.

'I'll see you later, Evie.'

'I'll be right here when you get back.'

You can count on that, sis, she silently added, watching her walk away, knowing she had so many years to make up for.

River, Dad's old dog, appeared from the shadows and trotted up to her. She smiled and gave him a stroke. Stayed there, petting him long after Lindy had cleared away the untouched food. The courage to walk the halls of the house non-existent. Which was ridiculous. It wasn't a living and breathing threat. And yet it felt like one.

She looked down at River. 'What's wrong with me, hey?'

River cocked his head with a whine.

'You're right, I should get it over with.'

Together they headed back inside. The hallway was deserted, her bags too had gone, and she felt the chilling emptiness of the house to her very bones.

She couldn't remember a time when it had been so quiet. She couldn't even hear Lindy. Just the patter of River's paws on the wood, the pad of her own bare feet. She wandered through the rooms, the kitchen, the dining room, the lounge, the family room, refusing to pause until she came upon the piano room. And there she froze.

She clutched a hand to her throat. Eyed the luxurious white carpet, the opulent chandelier that cast light around the room even when it wasn't on, and the magnificent bar that was worthy of the finest hotel. She could almost see her father there now mixing a drink, while Mum played a classical sonata at the piano, and she and her sisters sneaked down the hall to the cinema room and the popcorn machine. Loading up on sugar while Mum and Dad had their time…

Their time. Something they'd always carved out and something Eve had forgotten about until now…

Didn't mean it was love though. Real and true.

She squeezed her eyes shut and turned away. Opened them again to see her father's study door glaring back at her. Heavy, dark and taunting. She dragged in a breath. She had no desire to cross that threshold.

'Come on, River, it's time to find my own space in this hellhole.'

She headed to the other end of the house, to the bedrooms and her own. Expecting it to remain unchanged like the rest of the house but unable to stop the way her skin prickled as she stepped inside and saw she was right.

The same white and gold baroque-style furnishings, pale pink walls, white cotton bedspread, fluffy pink throw and matching pillows, so OTT but everything she'd wanted as a child.

And then she saw it. The bundle of neatly folded clothing at the bottom of the bed, an old Akubra resting on top…

She crossed the room, reached out with fingers that quivered like her heart. Mum's Akubra? She could see her now, smiling out from beneath its rim. Eyes warm and loving and… *Oh, Mum!*

She clutched it to her chest and a note fell to the floor. She dipped to pick it up…

Ride Jade.
She's perfect for you.
Rose x
PS Mum's hat is yours.
Take care of it, as it takes care of you!

She smiled, eyes welling, words blurring as she read it again, hovering over the 'x'.

'Oh, Rose.'

A kiss. Rose had given her a kiss. Not just that, she'd come in from the paddocks to welcome her home. She'd chosen the pool room to give her breathing space. She'd sorted out clothing without Eve having to ask for it. And they'd talked, properly talked.

Maybe they weren't so broken after all...

She pressed a kiss to the note, her resolve building with her love for her sister. They might not agree on the past, or her father, but they did agree on the future.

And Eve would fix it.

She would.

Come Monday she'd stride into Harrington Law and have it out with George. See to it that the man saw this whole situation as the nonsense it was.

Until then—she scooped up jeans and a shirt off the pile—there was a horse with her name on it...

CHAPTER FIVE

NATE DIDN'T HATE MONDAYS.

He was one of a rare breed that relished the start of a new week, fresh with possibility and the gains that could be made.

This Monday, however, he would gladly give it up as a bad job.

He'd got up, done his morning run, grabbed a shower, a coffee, and a breakfast bagel and hit the office for eight. Just as he would in Sydney. Only here, it was his father's office, he was sitting in his father's chair, and he might as well have had his father sitting over him for the suffocating tension in the air.

He twisted in his leather seat, rolled his head on his shoulders, and tried to ignore his surroundings that were stuck somewhere in the eighties. Wood panelled walls, retro colour scheme, even an avocado-coloured phone that had a cord, of all things…

None of which should impact his ability to do the job. And still he struggled. He was supposed to be looking into Holt Waverly's daughters, making a note of their contact details so that he could get in touch and introduce himself. Instead, his mind kept circling back to the family dinner he'd endured the night before.

Perhaps if he called his mother and apologised, he could put it to bed and get some work done. But apologising meant he was in the wrong. Not his father.

And he wasn't willing to go there.

Not when it was Dad who'd picked the fight. Who'd accused him of being distracted and caring more for the swanky city than his hometown. For thinking himself above Marni and its people. For staying away so long because he saw himself as better than his own family.

And how wrong could one man be?

Perhaps he should have fought back, told his father the truth. That the reason he was so distracted came down to a woman he'd met on Friday night in the very town he criticised him for hating.

And that the reason he'd stayed away all this time wasn't down to Marni, or its people, but his father himself.

That would've wiped the smug look of judgement off his face. An outright attack, laying the blame where it truly belonged. But the argument that would've ensued with his mother as a witness…after all the effort she'd put into making the evening special. No. Just no.

Far better to walk away and see to it that he saw his mother alone next time… He'd send her flowers. That would help. Flowers and a promise to take her to lunch later in the week. Better.

As for the striking city swan who'd wandered into his life, stirred it up and walked straight back out again, she'd made her thoughts clear and he should be grateful. She wasn't the woman for him, no matter the crazy connection. They were on opposite ends of the spectrum when it came to their lives and what they wanted from them.

Didn't stop him thinking about her though. Wondering. Wanting. Wishing...

When what you should be doing is focusing on the job!

He had four sisters in three different countries to speak to. One was recently wed—to royalty no less. That left the other three to comply and, as ridiculous as it sounded, their love lives or lack thereof far outweighed his own...

He was picking up the phone to dial Rose, Holt's eldest daughter, when his office door flew open and in strode...

'Eve!'

'Nate!'

Eve froze to the spot. She must be seeing things.

Her lurid dreams of the weekend making her conjure up the man who had filled them because it wasn't possible. It couldn't be. *He* couldn't be.

Yet she knew him. Her body *knew* him. Every inked stretch beneath the dark suit trousers, crisp white shirt and skinny black tie...

'I'm so sorry, Mr Harrington, she just barged right on in!' The disgruntled receptionist hurried up alongside her, her tiny form a blot in Eve's rapidly blurring vision. Of all the men in the world she had to walk in on, she had to—

Her brain halted, rewound. The receptionist had said, 'Mr Harrington'. *He* was Mr Harrington.

'It's okay, Penny. You can stand down. Eve and I are good friends.'

Good friends—*really?*

And if he was a Harrington, where was the other one? The older, less distracting one. The one she needed. And exactly what relation were they if he was a Harrington too? Surely not his...she swallowed...*son*?

'Oh. I see.' Penny gave her the once over, her heavily wing-tipped eyes narrowed with suspicion, her pillar-box-red pixie cut adding to her don't-mess-with-me air. 'In that case, can I bring you both some coffee?'

Nate smiled at Eve. 'Would you like some?'

'Some what?'

His eyes sparkled. 'Some coffee?'

'Would I—? No, I don't want coffee.' Coffee reminded Eve of Saturday morning, of being all cosy in his bed, an image that wasn't helping her come back down to earth. And why wasn't he as freaked out as she was by this unexpected encounter?

'We're good, thank you, Penny.'

He waited for the other woman to leave before

stepping around the desk. 'I wasn't expecting to see you again quite so soon.'

'I wasn't expecting to see you again ever.'

The corners of his mouth twitched. Did he find this *funny*?

'That's brutal.'

'It's the truth.'

'The brutal truth. And yet, here you are...' he swept a casual hand around him '...in my office of all places, tracking me down?'

'What—? No! I thought this was George Harrington's office. I'm here to *see* George.'

He frowned. 'Sorry to disappoint but my father is now retired. As of last week, I'm the new face of Harrington Law.'

'You're not!'

His frown twitched.

'I assure you I am.' He offered out his hand. 'Nate Harrington at your service.'

'You're a *lawyer*?'

She was deflecting from the hand he still held out, deflecting from the entire awkward, discombobulating, unbelievable situation! Instead she sounded as if she was questioning his ability to do the job altogether.

'Is that so hard to believe?'

'No, I just...' Words failed her.

'I was an equity partner at Spectre Cowan based in Sydney. This is now my firm. You can look up my credentials if you so wish.'

She shook her head—equity partner. Spectre

Cowan. Huge business. Impressive. She'd tell him as much if she weren't still reeling....

She eyed his hand and felt her fingers twitch, knowing what the contact would do to her, and forced herself to comply. They needed to get on a professional footing asap. The undercurrent had to be dismissed as an inconvenient rush. Friday night, Saturday morning, ever more so!

Though knowing him like she did...perhaps it was a good thing. An aid to her cause, so to speak.

'Eve.' She shook his hand, ignored the way the contact zipped along her veins, the way his gaze seared her. Warm and enticing. 'Though your father knows me as Evelyn. Evelyn Waverly.'

His hand pulsed around hers, eyes widening. 'Eve—Evelyn! How could I not have—? *You're* Holt's daughter.'

'Eve, please. Evelyn makes me think of my father. And yes, second eldest, for my sins.'

They were still bonded together, palm to palm, gazes locked.

She remembered what she'd told him in the bar. What he'd told her in return, about family and work bringing him back. Of his intention to stay if things worked out how he intended. Why hadn't she dug deeper? Realised who he was sooner? Done anything but slept with the one man who held her life in his hands.

'I thought you were in England.'

'Most people think I am and that's the way I'd like it to stay for as long as possible.'

'You look nothing like I expected.'

She balked. 'And what did you expect?'

'I'm not sure I should answer that.'

'Why?'

'For fear it could incriminate me.'

The tension eased a fraction. 'Like the "guess my name" game.'

'Pretty much.'

She laughed against her will and brought herself up sharp. She had a job to do and getting carried away on the connection wasn't getting it done. She released his hand and stepped away, clearing her throat. 'I never knew George had a son.'

'Doesn't surprise me.' He gave her a wry smile and settled back against the edge of his desk. 'My father never was one to talk about his family.'

'But you didn't come to any functions at the station?'

'When I was younger, my father didn't want the distraction, and when I was older, he didn't want the embarrassment.'

He stated it matter-of-fact. No emotion. No pain. But she felt the ache of his words deep within her chest. Knew how it felt. The station always came first at Garrison Downs, less home, more work HQ. So much so she'd feared being in the way as a kid, always falling over her own feet and causing unintentional trouble for Dad. And then she'd been a horrid reminder of the past, distracting her father from his perfect life ...someone to be shushed, kept out of sight, out of mind and she'd cultivated that, *wanting* to hurt him.

'Now *that* I can understand...'

He tilted his head, eyes sweeping over her. 'I got the impression that Holt doted on his daughters—you were his pride and joy?'

'No. Rose was his pride and Matilda was his joy. There wasn't a lot left for me.' She lifted her chin. 'Not that I cared in the end. I fared much better without him in my life.'

A shadow chased across his face. 'And it seems our conversation Friday night has come full circle.'

'You remember all of that.'

'I remember everything, Eve.'

His eyes torched her from within, the urge to close the distance between them and lose herself in that look hard to resist.

'Now it seems we're in messy territory.'

'Messy?' she said.

'As Holt's daughter, you're effectively my client and I don't make a habit of sleeping with the people I represent.'

She swallowed. Good. No sex. No confusion. No muddying the waters. 'You'll hear no argument from me.'

'I don't know whether to be offended or relieved.'

'How about both?' Fighting talk. Better. Much better.

He chuckled. 'Disappointed, too.'

She gave an edgy laugh, ignored the way his honesty cut effortlessly through her armour.

'If I told you I have nine months to get married, might that help take the edge off?'

She expected him to laugh with her, give some indication that the idea was as ludicrous as it felt, question it even. Instead, he fell silent.

'You know about it, don't you…? I mean, of course you do. Your father would have filled you in.'

'He did.' His nod was grave, all sign of humour gone. 'As his most important client and closest friend, my father ensured I was up to speed on all matters Holt Waverly related the second I returned. My first job today was to reach out to each of you, offer my condolences and introduce myself.'

'Right. Well, as you've probably surmised, I don't need the condolences and, as I'm acting on behalf of us all, let me save you some calls too and we'll get straight down to business.'

His eyes narrowed. 'Which is?'

'How you help us get out of it.'

'Out of it?'

'Yes. Surely you of all people can see why a condition requiring that any heiress marry to inherit is absurd and has no place in today's world.'

'It has a place,' he said, without hesitation, 'because it's in your father's will.'

Was he for real?

He looked genuine. Leaning back against his desk, arms now crossed, face as serious as one could be. But surely not?

'And we can just as easily write it out again,' she tried, 'yes?'

'No.'

Eve folded her arms, spine tightening. 'What do you mean, *no*?'

He returned to his seat behind the desk and gestured to the chair opposite. 'Why don't you take a seat?'

'I'd rather stand.'

Because confronting Harrington Senior about the marriage clause had been one thing. Confronting the man she'd slept with as recently as Saturday morning was something else…

'I don't know what you want me to say, Eve. Your father's last will and testament states quite clear that all women of marrying age must be wed within twelve months of the will reading. There's no debate.'

'*I'm* debating it. Right here. Right now.'

She couldn't keep the panic out of her voice, the anger too. Whether it was the ticking time clock, hearing him say it, hearing him say it without any understanding or compassion for what she and her sisters were going through, or the way he still made her feel…she didn't like it. Not one bit.

'How can you say it like it's okay?'

'My father has entrusted me with his work and that includes watching over you and your sisters and seeing to it that the clause is met.'

'Even if it's unjust, sexist, *insane*…?'

He leaned back in his seat, steepled his fingers together.

Cool. Calm. Collected.

Everything she wanted to be…

'Tell me something, Eve. There's clearly no love lost between you and your late father. And as I remember it, you're counting down the days until you can escape…'

'I am.'

'So why are you so het up about the inheritance? Financially you're already taken care of by your mother's trust and—'

'This isn't about me. This is about my sisters and what's fair. The station is Rose's life, she was born to take it on, and she should be the one to pass it on to her children, and her children's children. Not have it ripped out from under her because she isn't of the right *sex*.'

'Okay, so what do you want from me?'

She bit back her rising temper. 'Isn't it obvious?'

'Enlighten me…'

'I want you to find a loophole. I want you to help us out of it. I want you to give us legal advice and stop being so irritatingly cool about it.'

'Have you considered just doing it?'

'Doing *what*?'

'Finding yourself a man, drawing up a prenup, something I can help with and—'

'Are you *serious*?'

'Quite.'

She gawked at him. This was crazy, as crazy as…

'Hang on...' She thrust out a hand, her gut twisting with the sickening conclusion she was rapidly coming to. 'Did you know all along?'

'Know what?'

'Who I was? Is this all an act? Did you *sleep* with me because you knew and wanted *in*?'

He shot forward in his seat. 'You can't be serious.'

Finally, a reaction!

'Can't I? You're the one telling me to put a ring on it like it's the easiest thing in the world.'

'And you think I engineered our night together in the hope it would put me in the running. That I would withhold my identity and pretend I didn't *know* you, share the night with you, bring you breakfast...'

'Be all sweet—yes!'

'Because I want your inheritance?'

'Yes! You wouldn't be the first man to swindle his way into money and you wouldn't be the last.'

'Person.'

'What?'

'The first *person*. Or are you truly as sexist as you sound?'

'In my experience, men are the weaker sex, far more likely to be led around by their...' She twirled a finger at his desk, her target clear, and swallowed the inconvenient rush making a return. 'That and their greed.'

'Wow, your father really did do a number on you.'

The fire within her promptly died and the blood seeped from her cheeks.

'No, Eve,' he said coolly. 'I can assure you, had I known who you were when I met you, I would have steered well clear.'

Her heart winced and she straightened against it, clung to the common sense telling her she was right to fight. 'Scared of the gossip, the speculation that you lured me in?'

'No.'

'Then why?'

'Because as you said yourself…' he was back on his feet, walking towards her, blue eyes raging a storm '…you have no intention of getting serious. Not now. Not ever.'

He was repeating her words back at her, only they felt colder, harsher from his lips.

'You have no desire for love, and I have *all* the desire for it.'

'You couldn't know that before speaking to me,' she whispered, breathless with his increasing proximity, his reasoning too.

'No. That's true enough. But I do know, and so you should know this in return.' He paused a stride away. 'When I marry, Eve, it will be because I cannot bear to live without that woman by my side, because I love her and I want to spend the rest of my life with her.'

She gave a chilling laugh. 'How very noble of you.'

'It's not noble. It's natural. As natural as breathing. Craving love and giving it in return is what we were born to do.'

Emotions clogged up her throat, words difficult to form. 'How can you say that after the way your father treated you?'

'Because my father taught me how not to love and my mother gave it in abundance. She never tires of dishing it out and I won't either.'

His words snaked through her, making her want and making her want to recoil. Contrary and dizzying with it.

'If you're truly up to speed on my father and the inheritance, you must know my father was unfaithful to my mother and that I have a sister we never knew existed. He kept her from us. What kind of a man cheats on his wife, fathers a child and then refuses to bring that child into the family?'

'A man who's trying to protect that family.'

'We didn't *need* his protection. We needed his honesty.'

'And now you have it.'

'Too much too late. What good is it now? When all those years have been lost?'

'What's done is done, Eve.'

She gave a choked laugh, shook her head. 'You don't understand.'

'I understand more than you know and I'm telling you, don't let the past destroy your future.'

Now he sounded like Rose. 'My future would be just fine if you could hand me a way out of this.'

'Your future isn't fine, not while you think it's

okay to project your father's behaviour onto others, onto me…'

'I'm not projecting.'

'No?'

She took an unsteady breath, the fight dying within her. 'Look, I didn't come here to fight… well, I did, but not about this. I wanted help, a way out for me and my sisters.'

She held his gaze, pleading with him to understand.

'Surely you can see it from our position, from mine. I don't want to be forced to take vows I cannot keep.'

'Who says you can't keep them?'

'I do. I won't marry for convenience and I won't marry for love. The former is a lie and the latter is too fickle.'

'If that's truly how you feel, then you need to accept that Garrison Downs will return to its original owner. It was your ancestor's wish.'

'But it's a part of us now, it's a part of Rose. She can't lose it.'

'Then as far as I see it, you have only one option, Eve.'

'Which is?'

'Find yourself a husband.'

Have you heard yourself? came Nate's inner conscience. *She may have made some nasty assumptions about you and lashed out, but she's cornered and asking you for help.*

And she was right. It was archaic and sexist… but no more sexist than she was being.

And if he was honest with himself. There had been a moment. A split second of inexplicable madness where he'd felt her desperation deep within his gut and thought, why not him?

Plenty of people married for a lot less.

But he wasn't in the plenty.

He wanted love.

And she wanted her life in London back, her job that by her own words was her life. She was his father through and through.

'I don't believe this.' She threw her hands in the air and paced away. 'You know, for a man who talked so much sense on Friday night, you aren't making any now.'

'I'm making perfect sense.'

'Really?' she threw over her shoulder.

'If you're not bothered about love, then why not get married to someone, a friend, an acquaintance, someone who understands your situation. I can ensure you're protected with a prenup, the other party too, because as far as I'm aware, but I'd need to double-check, there's no time constraint on that marriage. Nothing that demands you *stay* married. You could be a free heiress within another year.'

She paused before the window. Quiet.

'Eve?'

'I'm… I'm thinking.'

'What is there to think about? You secure your

part in the inheritance and go back to your life in London. It's a win-win.'

He'd be one step closer to satisfying his promise to his father too.

And yet he felt cold at the prospect.

'It's a lie, is what it is.'

'Newsflash, Eve, people lie all the time.'

'Some do it easier than others.'

And he knew she was speaking of her father, her shoulders hunched as she hugged her middle.

'I'm sorry for what your father put you through.' He walked up behind her, careful to maintain a safe distance, one from which he could resist the need to touch her. 'And I'm sorry you struggle to trust. But I promise you, I didn't lie on Friday and I'm not lying to you now.'

She turned into him, her perfume lifting with the movement and transporting him back to that night when they'd been as close as any couple could be. When they'd been on the same side of the fence, waging war against their fathers. United by that bond.

'I had no idea who you were,' he said into her eyes that swirled with so much emotion he could feel his resolve crumbling. 'All I knew is that from the moment I saw you step out of that cab, I wanted to get to know you and the more I learned, the more I wanted you.'

And he felt it now, the power of it, the desire… an innate lure that he was struggling to smother.

'Then tell me something else…' she whispered.

'What?'

'Do you want me now?'

He cursed. The lie impossible to give. The truth impossible to act on.

'Because I want you, Nate.' She wound the end of his tie around her fist, eased him closer and he could scarce believe the change in her, let alone the thrilling heat streaking through his body. 'And that terrifies me as much as it energises me. I've never met anyone who can empty my head with a simple look…but you do.'

'And you, me.' The words were out before he could stop them, her coy smile worth every weakened second of his confession.

'Then please…' she wet her lips '…help me out of it.'

Ice flooded his veins. *Legal assistance.* That was what she truly wanted. Not him. Not this. Just a way out.

'Clever, Eve.' He grabbed her wrist. 'Very clever.' And he was a fool.

She frowned. 'I don't know what you—'

'I will help you *through* this, Eve. But I can't get you out of it. I swore to my father I would take care of you and your sisters and see the terms of the will met. And that is what I'll do.'

Her eyes shot daggers, her cheeks flushed deep. 'Why play the dutiful son to a father who doesn't deserve it?'

'Because I can, and I think deep down you wish you could too.'

Her lashes fluttered, her mouth falling open. It was a low blow but he feared her bitterness, her inability to make amends with the past. There was so much anger in her, so much hurt. It was high time she faced it head-on. The loss and what it meant for her, for the relationship she would never get to repair.

'You think I care that he's gone?' It came out tight, her eyes burning bright, their sheen telling him more than she ever would.

'I think you care more than you want to admit, and the sooner you accept it, the better for all those around you.'

'I didn't hear you complaining about my company Friday night.'

'Friday night you held your cards close to your chest, but it was still there, eating away at you beneath the careful veneer.'

She fought against his words, his hold, his gaze. Locked in a fierce battle, blue eyes piercing blue, her glossy lips parted but nothing coming out.

He wanted to kiss her. Kiss her until lust took out the pain. Kiss her until she could admit her grief. Kiss her until she let the tears fall and she could be reborn. That bit brighter, that bit freer.

And what a weird fantasy that was…

'Now I suggest you leave before we end up where you almost had us.'

'What makes you think…?'

He lowered his gaze to where the delicate fabric of her blouse betrayed her body's desire and she snatched her hand out of his grasp, gripped it before her chest.

'Why, you...'

He gave a tight chuckle because, for all he was teasing her for feeling it, he felt it too. A hundred times over.

'You said it yourself, Eve, and, like me, you're no liar.'

She stared back at him hard. 'Fine! You won't help us. I'll find someone who will.'

'You do that. And when you find him, I'll be right here waiting with a prenup.'

'That's not what I meant.'

'So you say...'

She opened her mouth, closed it again, made a noise akin to a growl and spun away. She yanked open his door, giving him one last murderous glance...

Hell, she was hot when she was angry. Something else she'd hate hearing and he would take too much delight in saying.

And then she was gone and he was no better off than he had been Saturday morning, only then they'd parted on polite terms, and it had been wishful thinking that he'd see her again. Now he *knew* he'd see her again.

See her again and see her married off too. But the idea of Eve getting married to someone else...

Nate had never thought of himself as the jealous kind.

It seemed his gut thought otherwise.

* * *

'Why, of all the pig-headed, egotistical, arrogant...'

Eve stormed through the station, doors slamming in her wake as she headed straight for the bar. She paused outside the piano room just long enough to slip off her shoes before crossing Mum's precious white carpet and resuming her stomping.

'Hey, what's all the racket?'

She didn't turn at Rose's question. Though she was surprised her sister was around. 'What are you doing here? Shouldn't you be out there still...?'

She waved a careless hand to the outdoors as she spied her drink of choice and plucked both bottle and glass off the shelf, setting them down with a satisfying clink against the marble.

'Are you trying to break everything?'

'I'm trying to work my frustration out of my system. Is that okay, Boss?'

Rose gave a tired laugh.

'What's so funny?'

'It's been a long time since I've heard you call me that.'

Eve harrumphed as she plonked some ice into her glass and poured herself a decent measure. 'Clearly this place is getting to me.'

'In a good way, I hope.'

'So long as you don't start calling me Bambi, I'd say we're okay.'

Rose leaned into the door frame, careful to keep her body angled outwards and her dust-covered workwear away from the carpet. 'I never understood why you took such issue with being called it. We always thought it was endearing.'

'Button was endearing. And Boss was to be admired,' Eve said, referring to their father's pet names for Matilda and Rose, respectfully. 'But *Bambi*?'

'You just saw the bad in it.' Her sister's expression turned wistful. 'You didn't see that it was because you were adorable, with your big doe eyes and sweet smile.'

'You forgot my spindly legs,' Eve said, taking a nerve-quenching swig, 'and my habitual ability to fall over my own feet.'

'All cute.'

Eve shook her head, her laugh unsteady with the past, the sentiment, the sentiment in Rose, too. Maybe there was something in what her sister said, but the man wasn't here to ask. Just as Nate had so kindly reminded her...

'So...' she said, ignoring the wound doing its best to open up and focusing on her sister, who looked increasingly beat. 'You want one of these too? Because you look like you could do with it.'

'You're kidding, right? The day's going to be long enough as it is. Alcohol isn't going to help.'

'It dulls the pain though.' Eve took another ice-clinking swig and joined her sister on the threshold. 'So why are you here instead of out there?'

Rose rubbed her brow. 'I had some calls I needed to make. I have three jackaroos down with a bug at the worst possible time and I need to lean on our neighbours for help…'

'Isn't everyone busy this time of year?'

'They are, hence the personal calls. If we don't get the yards processed asap we'll be up the proverbial creek without a paddle.'

'Is it that bad?'

'It is when we've more pregnant heifers than we've had in years due to the recent rains, now a heatwave to boot, and I want them out the yards as soon as possible. We've yet to ear-tag the calves and the trucking company is demanding I grade two roads at the southern boundary before they'll drive in. Like I said, the proverbial creek.'

With every word, Eve felt her guilt swell. Her sense of uselessness too. Something she hadn't felt in years. Not since she'd left this place.

Less than a week in and Garrison Downs had her regressing.

Calling Rose 'Boss'. Feeling inferior, useless, a spare part…and getting nowhere with the one task she had been assigned.

'Can I do anything?'

'You are doing something.' Rose smiled. 'You're getting us out of this marriage clause.'

Of all the things her sister could've said…

'I meant with the station, with the mustering?'

Rose's mouth quirked. 'Are you offering to saddle up?'

Eve gave a cautious shrug. 'Why not? My roping skills might be rusty but I'm sure I'll get the hang of it again.'

Rose's gaze drifted over Eve's silk blouse, pencil skirt, daintily painted toenails before returning to rest on Eve's hand around her glass.

'That manicure won't last a second.'

'There are more manicures to be had...' She waggled the fingers of her free hand and Rose chuckled.

'You're serious?'

'I wouldn't offer if I wasn't. Just put me to work, Boss.'

And if she was working, hopefully Rose wouldn't ask how her other task was going because right now she didn't have an answer. Other than Nate's.

Find yourself a husband.

How the man had the audacity to even stand there and *suggest* it...

Rose gave a sudden frown. 'You're sure?'

'Huh?'

'You just turned the air blue.'

'I did what?'

Rose cocked a brow. 'You swore...'

'It's all the excitement.'

'If you say so...' Rose's eyes danced, clearly torn between laughing and biting her hand off. 'Okay then, you'd best go get yourself changed. We're heading through the ravine to the east and, thanks to the rains, it's extra boggy.'

She gave a mock shudder. 'Wet *and* dirty—my favourite.'

'You'll do just fine, Bambi.'

'Don't! Please!' But Eve didn't feel the customary prick of bitterness with the name. All she felt was the warmth of Rose's love. 'You know, I think I preferred it when we weren't really speaking.'

'And I think I preferred it when you were a shy and retiring bookworm, but we can't all have what we want, can we?' Rose grinned. 'Now, get yourself off, we're setting off in ten.'

Eve was already moving.

'Oh, wait a sec!' Rose called after her. 'How did the meeting go?'

So much for escaping it...

Slowly, she turned, took in Rose's hopeful gaze and forced a smile.

'It went. George Harrington has retired. Seems you were right about his health. We're dealing with his son now.'

'His *son*? I didn't know George had a son.'

'Neither did I.'

'How was he?'

'*He* was a pig-headed, egotistical, arrogant arse.' The truth flowed from her lips with surprising force and she realised she couldn't lie to Rose about their situation. She was done keeping stuff from her sisters when it affected them as much as her...though she'd keep the sex to herself. *No one* needed to know about that.

'You do have a lovely way with words, Evie.'

'It's my job.' She downed the rest of her drink. 'As for his job...you'd think his age would make him more sympathetic to our cause, instead he's quite the opposite. Committed to seeing us abide by the ancient nonsense our ancestors have dished out.'

'Hence the tantrum when I came in?'

'I wasn't having a tantrum. I was venting.'

Rose surprised her with a grin. 'He really got to you, didn't he?'

'I wouldn't be grinning about it, Rose.'

'I'm grinning because he doesn't know what he's in for, having you as enemy. I'm just glad you're on my side.'

Now Eve smiled, the sisterly camaraderie boosting her when she'd feared her news would set Rose back further.

'Always. Now let me go so I can get out of my finest and plough my frustration into something useful…'

And forget about the way a certain pair of blue eyes and inked skin made her feel.

Especially when they belonged to the man so determined to see her and her sisters marched up the aisle, she was surprised he hadn't got the shotgun out.

Then again, shotgun weddings implied something else entirely.

And that thought was about as unhelpful and disturbing as the man himself.

CHAPTER SIX

WORKING FOR ROSE, with Rose, did work to an extent.

While the bug did its rounds within the bunk-house, Eve filled the role of a jillaroo with as much effort and determination as she did her PR role in London. Though nothing about this job was glamorous or image focused, it didn't exhaust her creative brain to the point that she struggled some days to tell the lie she'd spun from the truth.

And it was liberating.

It had even been kind of fun, getting stuck back into station life…a life she hadn't wanted to be a part of any more, but it seemed without the destructive secret, that life wasn't quite done with her.

If her colleagues back in London could see her now, they wouldn't recognise her. Hair loosely tied back, dust motes making a home in her costly honey-eyed strands, her make-up-free cheeks flushed with colour from the outdoors. Kitted out, rough and ready. But as she looked out over the land, the sun setting behind the mountains and casting an orange glow over the dirt that didn't look quite so dirty any more…she found she didn't care.

'What's that smile about?' Rose asked, stepping onto the deck with two coldies in hand and offering one out.

'Thanks. I was just wondering what my colleagues in London would make of me now.'

Rose gave a soft laugh as Eve took a swig from the bottle and almost brought it straight back up. Odd, the bitterness was hitting her all wrong. She checked the date on the bottle as Rose joined her on the swing seat.

'In my opinion, you look good for it, Evie.'

Did she? Or was Rose just being kind? Probably, a bit of both but she was happy enough to take it.

They settled back into the cushions, Rose gently rocking the seat with her heel as Eve let the warmth of the setting sun soothe every aching limb. There was something to be said for a hard day's labour and being able to bask in the rest. Something blissful and satisfying.

'Have you heard any more from Harrington Junior?'

And just like that she stiffened. 'No.'

Because although she'd managed to push Nate out by day, rejecting every attempt he'd made to contact her, her nights were filled with him. Dreams she couldn't control. Thoughts that would wander when she lay awake, work unable to distract her.

'How did you leave it when you saw him in Marni?'

Eve huffed into her beer and promptly lowered

it. Its scent made her stomach roll. Or was it Nate and the way he'd managed to get under her skin?

'Honest answer—he said we should get ourselves husbands with an expiry date.'

She expected Rose to laugh or at least be as cross as she was.

But she was quiet. Contemplative.

'You're not seriously considering it?'

'I won't lie, Evie, the thought has occurred to me, too.'

'You are joking!'

'Would it really be so bad if it got us what we want?'

'Please tell me you're joking…'

But of course her sister wasn't joking…this was precisely the reason Eve had come home. To ensure her sister didn't do something so drastic to keep it.

But hearing her *say* it.

'I don't know.' Rose shrugged. 'Marriage for a set period and then being able to move on with our lives without this hanging over us, I can't deny the appeal.'

'*Appeal?* Have you heard yourself?'

'I know, but I'm tired, Evie. Physically. Mentally. And what am I without this place?'

'You're a wonderful woman who deserves so much more than a forced marriage of convenience that wasn't of your choosing.'

'I *choose* this place, though.'

'I know.' And Eve did know, it was what worried her so much.

'Have you come up with a better idea in the month you've been here?'

Eve's heart launched into her throat. A *month*.

'Has it really been a month?'

'Time flies when you're having fun, right?'

'Yeah…' Though Eve wasn't really listening. She was doing the maths. A month equated to four weeks. Twenty-eight days and she hadn't had a period.

And she was as regular as clockwork.

And… She raised the bottle to her lips, got the same whiff that sent her stomach churning.

No. *No*, she couldn't be.

'You want a Pinot Grigio instead?' Rose said, spying her distaste. 'We have plenty of Mum's old favourite.'

'No—no, I'm not in the mood.'

'Really?' Rose frowned, scrutinising Eve's face. 'Are you okay?'

'I'm fine.'

'You really don't look so fine any more.'

'Can you manage without me in the morning?'

'Of course,' her sister said, frown deepening. 'How come?'

'I need to pop into town.'

'You're going to try again with Harrington Junior?'

Eve gulped—sickness, unease, panic all rising up. 'You never know.'

'So long as you remember this isn't all on you, Evie. We each have a role to play, whether it's getting out of it or not. But I'm glad of it for one thing. It brought you back home, and for that I'm grateful.'

Eve's smile quivered, her sister's love battling against the inner panic.

'Me too, Rose,' she whispered, taking her sister's hand and giving it a squeeze. Because she was. She had her sister back. Had found a place within the station again. But a baby. Pregnant. *Her*.

Tomorrow, she would buy a test, many tests… and then she would know for sure.

Though she suspected she already knew.

'This is incredibly sweet of you, Mrs Cooper, but it's really not necessary.'

'Nonsense!' the old woman said, shoving the Victoria sponge at him and giving Nate no choice but to take it. 'With all the help your father gave us over the years, it's the least I can do. You know, if it hadn't been for him after my Charlie had fallen off that ladder and his company refused to pay out, I don't know where we'd be now.'

'So you've said.'

Several times over now. And Mrs Cooper wasn't the only 'client' to swing by and tell him stories of his father's generosity, and bring gifts, mainly of the richly unhealthy variety. No wonder his father's health had taken a severe turn for the worse if he ate like this on a regular basis.

'But, you see, it was your father who insisted he represent us. We couldn't afford it. He took all the risk, did all the work and only took a fraction of what he was due. He was a godsend.'

A godsend. He'd heard his father called that many times over too. Or words to that effect. All of them effusive, all of them bearing no resemblance to the man he'd been brought up by.

And he wasn't surprised their views differed because his father's focus had always been on work, work and his clients, but these people weren't *paying* clients. Not in the way Holt and his peers were.

This was pro bono.

The time it would have taken. Time when he'd resented his father for caring more about money and business than his own family.

Had he been wrong to judge his father so harshly?

But then how could he judge him any different—*know* any different—when his father had never been around?

With a tight smile, he acknowledged Mrs Cooper's praise. 'I'll be sure to pass on your regards.'

'You see that you do.'

'Now, is there anything I can help you with?'

'Oh, no, not at all.' She gave him an eye-crinkling grin and reached out to pat his hand. 'I was just passing and wanted to introduce myself. It's good to know you're here filling his extra-big shoes. We're sure to be safe in Harrington hands.'

'That you are, Mrs Cooper. Now I really must get back to work.'

Actual work because the past few weeks had

been dominated by Mrs Coopers wanting to feed him up while waxing lyrical about his father. Probing mothers assessing him as husband material for their daughters, and husbands sent in by their wives for the same. And don't get him started on the single ladies.

He ushered her towards the open door. 'Penny, can you see this cake is stored somewhere safe?' He slid it onto his receptionist's desk and they shared a look that said, *If this doesn't stop, gym membership will need to be added to the employee benefit scheme.*

'I'll pop some around to my father later,' he assured them both.

'Oh, that's a lovely idea.' Mrs Cooper beamed as he escorted her onto the street. 'He really is such a wonderful man, so kind and generous and thoughtful.'

'Goodbye, Mrs Cooper.'

He watched her amble away and scratched the back of his head. He was struggling to marry together the two versions of the man that was his father. Would have carried on debating it too if his senses hadn't prickled as a blonde woman stepped out of the pharmacy across the way.

Head down, face mostly hidden by a dusty Akubra. He couldn't see her features enough to identify her but there was something about her. Something that had him inexplicably drawn.

Maybe it was the hair. The way the golden hue caught the light as it fell in a loose ponytail at her nape. Or the way her tall and slender figure moved with the grace and confidence of a...*swan*.

Eve? But it couldn't be. Dressed as she was. Bootcut jeans, a flannel shirt tucked in at the waist, dusty work boots, the hat...and yet—

'Eve!'

Her name was out before he could think better of it. They'd hardly left things on good terms, and she'd ignored every call he'd made since. But as her lawyer, he needed to fix things. As her ex-lover, if you could call it that, he owed her much more.

Only, she wasn't slowing. She was speeding up, the paper bag she was carrying clutched to her chest.

No doubt in his mind now, he leaned inside the office. 'I'll be back shortly, Penny.'

And legged it after her, narrowly missing a battered Jeep that honked its horn. He waved an apology, tried again. 'Eve!'

He picked up his pace, caught up to her as she rounded a parked truck.

'Eve, wait, please!'

She yanked the door open, tossed the bag inside and he stepped forward, fearing she was about to follow it in when she slammed it closed again and leaned back against the metal. Silently, she lifted her head, blue eyes blazing out from beneath the rim of her Akubra.

'Look, I'm sorry for how we left things. I've been trying to get hold of you but—'

'I've been busy.'

'So I gather… Helping Rose with the station I take it?'

Because why else would she be dressed like so…

'And we're coping just fine, thank you.'

'I didn't doubt it. I'm just…' he swallowed, chose his words carefully '…surprised to see you looking so different.'

She cocked her head. 'You ran over here to comment on how I look?'

'No—no, of course not. I ran over here to apologise. I didn't want to hurt you, Eve. It was never my intention. I'd never have let things go so far if I'd known.'

'That makes two of us.'

'So if we agree on that, can we also agree to put it behind us and work together to move forward?'

'Are you ready to forgo your father's favour to help us?'

'It's not as easy as that.'

'No?'

'You don't understand.'

'What don't I understand? Because last I checked you didn't owe him anything.'

'It seems…' His eyes drifted to the front of Harrington Law, his head and heart at war with all that he had learned of late. 'You know how you think you've known someone all your life, like really known them, and then…' His eyes came back to hers that were spearing him, daring him to finish that thought. 'Of course, you do, I'm sorry.'

'And there I was thinking you were trying to dig

a deeper hole… So your father's not the man you thought either. This is my surprised face.'

He gave her a meek smile. 'I didn't mean to poke at an old wound.'

'Don't worry, this old wound has been opening up again ever since I returned.'

'Yeah, well, mine doesn't know whether it's opening or closing or taking on a whole new shape.'

Her nose wrinkled. 'This conversation has taken an icky turn.'

He gave a soft laugh, grateful for the slight thaw in her demeanour. 'Fathers and their hidden lives.'

'Mine had a whole other family, what was yours hiding from you?'

His mouth twisted up. 'When I came here, I thought I was taking on a shrinking business. Dad's big clients were going the way of your father and he wasn't replacing them.'

'Death becomes us all,' she said smoothly, though she wasn't as unaffected as she wanted him to believe. The flicker to her lashes giving her away, the defensive stance too as she crossed her arms.

'True.'

'I'm assuming this was your father's wind-down plan though. He wouldn't want to leave anyone in the lurch when he retired?'

'Again true, though he thought he had a few more years in him.'

'But life had other ideas…'

'Yes.'

'Hence your secondment.'

'It's more than a secondment.'

'So you say, though I find it hard to believe you can give up somewhere like Sydney for the back-waters of Marni.' She had the decency to look a little sheepish as she checked she hadn't been over-heard. 'It's not like it doesn't have a *certain* appeal, but compared to the hustle and bustle of the city, the life…?'

'I always intended to return one day, Eve, make a life here. I don't want a family in a place where I can't let my kids roam free for traffic and peo-ple. My—'

Her sudden pallor had him frowning, silencing his spiel.

'You were saying,' she said, her voice muted, her arms hugging her middle tighter.

What was wrong with her?

'Nate?'

He pressed on, still distracted by her reaction but determined to make her understand his life's ambition. 'My intention was to make Harrington Law into something deserving of my name over the door. I wasn't doing it to make my father proud. Work was everything to him and I set out to prove it didn't have to be. That I could have a success-ful business and, eventually, a family. The whole package. And I'd do it better than him, because I'd never neglect those that I love to achieve it.'

'It's a lovely ideal,' she whispered.

'It's more than an ideal, it's my future. One I'll

see happen, but I never envisaged my father playing any role in it. He was always so distant.'

'And now?'

'Now it seems my father isn't the man I thought, or he is, but there's another side to him, one I never saw...'

'And one that changes how you feel?'

'I don't know. All I know is that high-paying clients like Holt gave him the income to support those who couldn't afford his services. When he wasn't working for your father et al, he was working for the locals. Sometimes free of charge, sometimes to cover costs alone, sometimes in exchange for *cake*, but always working.'

Eve's mouth quirked up. 'Cake?'

'It would appear that way.'

'So your father was a modern-day Robin Hood minus the stealing?'

Nate pressed his lips together. 'Unless you count the hours he robbed from his own wife and son to be able to do all that. Yes, he was.'

Her eyes flitted over his face. 'I'm sorry. I know how much you resented his work growing up, but maybe this can help you understand why he did what he did. At least his motives were pure, altruistic even. No one can say that about mine.'

'I don't know. I'm fast learning that things aren't always as black and white as they seem. My father believed Holt to be an honourable man, a man who wasn't proud of what he did, but he did his best to make amends and look after all concerned.'

'By keeping Ana a secret?'

'Think about it, Eve. Your family was fragile back then. My father hasn't gone into much detail, but I do know that keeping Anastasia a secret was as much about keeping your family together as it was about doing the right thing by her and Lili.'

'Your father seems to know an awful lot about it.'

She lowered her head, hiding beneath her Akubra as she scuffed at the ground with her boot.

'You could talk to him if you think it would help.'

'Your father?' Her head shot up, her eyes clashing with his. 'It's not me who needs to talk to George, but you.'

'You wouldn't say that if you saw us in a room together.'

'Don't you think it would help to get it off your chest, to tell him how you felt growing up? Give him the chance to fix things while you still can?'

'Just because you regret not having it out with your father, it—'

'That's not what I regret.'

'It isn't?'

'No. I had it out with him. I had it out with him in front of my mother, too, but I never had the courage to stay and deal with the fallout, I didn't *want* to give him the opportunity to make amends, to explain away what he did. What I regret is all those years I could have had with my mother, my sisters... I don't know whether things could have been different with my father and I don't get to find out, but maybe you can tell me something?'

'What's that?'

'In all those conversations with your father, has there ever been any hint as to *why* they didn't do something about it?'

'The condition?'

'Yes.'

'I asked my father the same.'

'You *did* question it?'

He looked away. He couldn't lie to her but neither did he want to give her false hope.

'I was surprised to see the condition, yes. Surprised even more that my father and Holt hadn't tried to see it changed. Especially when it risks the land going back to the Garrisons.'

She cursed the name, reaffirming what he already knew about the mutual hatred between the two families.

'And what did he say, when you questioned it?'

'He said that the station was a huge responsibility and that he believed Holt didn't want his daughters shouldering it alone. My father believed your mother was your father's rock, that they were stronger together—'

'And look how he repaid her.'

'Eve, he was unfaithful, I know, but my father truly believes they came through that period stronger. Your mother was unwell and—'

'Don't. Don't go there.'

He hesitated but knew it wasn't his place. Talking hearsay on something so personal.

'That wasn't all my father had to say...'

'No?' She was wary now, he could sense it in her held breath, her stiffened shoulders.

'But these are my father's words, not Holt's.'

'Understood.'

Nate took a breath and recalled the conversation he'd had that very first day back in Marni. And now he knew more, especially where Eve was concerned, he realised there wasn't just 'something' in it, there was a lot.

'According to my father, Holt feared you sisters would never come together again.'

He paused, thinking she may say something—reject it, accept it. Nothing. Not even a blink of the eye.

'He was scared that Rose was too married to the land to ever find a husband to share the load with. Matilda would never leave. You would never come home. And as for Anastasia, she needed a reason to be brought into the fold, a reason that would bind you all together, something that requires you as sisters to come together for a single goal.'

Still, she said nothing. One second. Two. And then she laughed. Outright laughed.

'My God, your father is a soppy old fool.'

Nate frowned. 'Not the reaction I was expecting.'

'It's crazy. Fanciful. As fanciful as the clause itself!'

'But you've come back, haven't you? Not only that but you're changing. You're not the same woman who landed here a month ago. Visually. Physically.

Mentally. Even I can see that. And you're glowing, Eve.'

She also sounded less English, more Australian, but she already looked horrified enough by everything he'd said so he kept that to himself.

'You don't know what you're talking about.'

'Don't I?'

'No, you don't, and neither does your father. Or mine. If he truly felt that way. Rose doesn't need a man to run that land with her. I don't need a man to tie me to it. Tilly—well, it's just a fortunate mishap that she fell in love with a prince and has left for pastures new. And Ana…well, I don't know much about Ana yet, but I will, just as soon as I can get myself over to Melbourne to see her.'

'Which is when?'

'I don't know.'

'But you will see her?'

'Of course. She's my sister.'

He was smiling, he couldn't help it. Could she not see how much his father's supposition was ringing true?

'I hate to tell you, Eve, but this is hardly a convincing argument.'

Her cheeks coloured, her eyes flashed. 'You can say what you like, but you don't know us. You don't know Rose and how capable she is. If you spent one day at the station, you'd realise what a nonsense this all is.'

'Is that an offer?'

'Is what an offer?'

'Are you inviting me to spend a day at the station?'

She lifted her chin higher, her blue eyes shimmering in their intensity. 'It's a busy time of year and we're short-handed, I'm not sure now is the ideal time.'

'Surely the challenging circumstances *make* it the ideal time to prove what you say.'

Her throat bobbed.

'What are you so afraid of?'

'I'm not afraid.'

'You could have fooled me.'

'I'm *not* afraid.'

'Tomorrow, then. I'll see you and Rose tomorrow.'

'But I haven't checked with Rose.'

'Then check with Rose and let me know. Because I'm coming to visit, Eve, whether you like it or not.'

CHAPTER SEVEN

EVE PLACED THE stick down beside the steadily growing line of tests on her en suite sink.

Different brands, all with the same result.

Was it possible that they could all be wrong?

That the sticks and her body could *all* be wrong?

She pressed her fist to her mouth and knew the answer well enough. She really was pregnant and she hadn't a clue what to do about it. Which seemed to be the story of her life lately.

'Evie, you coming?' Rose hollered from down the hall. 'If we don't get out there now, we're going to be chasing our tails for the rest of the day.'

She hurried to scoop up the tests, fearing her sister was about to walk in, and tossed them in the pedal bin, pushing the sluggish lid closed.

She was supposed to be here to help. Supposed to be here chipping in with the work and seeing to it that Rose kept the station for evermore. Not making matters worse.

Before she'd at least had the *option* of finding herself a husband...

Now the only man she could even consider marrying was the baby's father. And, yes, she'd teased him, accused him even, of wanting exactly that, she hadn't *meant* it.

But then she hadn't meant to get pregnant either.

'Eve!'

'Coming!'

She raced from the room to find her sister pacing at the rear porch, gaze intent on a document in her hand. She glanced up as soon as she saw her. 'About time.'

'Sorry, Boss.' Eve dodged her eye as she tied her hair back. 'What's that?'

'Another report that needs filing.'

'Need a hand with it?' Eve took her Akubra off the rack, hiding her face beneath it as she shoved her feet into her boots.

'Nah.' Rose tossed the report aside, giving Eve her full attention as she tried to hurry past her. 'Hey, you feeling okay?'

Perspiration broke out over Eve's skin.

'I'm fine,' she said, without slowing, grateful for the fresh air that hit her as she stepped outside. She sucked in a lung full and kept on going.

'Have you had breakfast?' Rose called after her.

'Not hungry.'

'Evie, you need to eat.'

She threw her sister a look. 'Pot and kettle springs to mind.'

Rose plucked a paper bag off the boot bench and tossed it at her.

'What's this?'

'Breakfast.' Rose strode ahead of her and Eve peeked in the bag, grateful her sister couldn't see her face that was sure to look as green as she felt. The grease enough to have her tossing it into the nearby hedge.

She apologised to Mum's golden grevilleas, something wild would sure enjoy it later, paper and all, and continued after Rose. The horses were already saddled in the yard, the station hands well enough to work were gathered and the quadbike engines purred.

'You ate that quick,' Rose remarked as she checked the girth on Opal's saddle and Eve did the same with Jade. 'Are you sure you're—?'

'Rose!' Aaron hollered, unwittingly coming to Eve's aid. 'We've got a problem.'

'What now…?' Rose said under her breath as the guy jogged up to them, his tall and burly frame a silhouette against the sunrise.

'We have a bore pump down to the east and Jacko ain't fit to see to it.'

Rose cursed, pinched her nose.

'You go. Take Kylie with you.'

'But what about—?'

'It's fine, we'll manage.'

'How? You won't—'

'I said we'll manage.' Rose stared the big bloke down until he dipped his hat and left.

'Rose,' Eve said, 'don't we need Kylie on—?'

The roar of an approaching motorbike broke

through the bustle in the yard and Rose turned in its direction. 'Who on earth…?'

But Eve knew. Without looking she knew. Felt his presence like a sixth sense.

'Stay here.' Rose swung herself up into the saddle. 'I'm going to check who this is.'

And she was off before Eve could stop her. Stop her and explain. Because though she'd told Nate she would check and report back, she hadn't done either.

Call it denial, distraction, or whatever, she hadn't mentioned anything to Rose and now that he was upon them, she realised what a bad move that had been.

Eve mounted Jade, clicked her tongue and spurred her horse into following. She caught up with Rose just as her sister reached their unexpected visitor and she watched, helpless, as Nate cut the engine and tugged his helmet from his head, stealing Eve's breath in the process.

Didn't matter that she was well versed in how he looked, Nate in leathers with the soft glow of the dawning sun setting off his blue eyes, the bronze of his skin, his easy smile…he was something else.

He was also the father of the child within her…

Jade shimmied to the left as her hold on the reins slackened and she straightened, tightened her grip…wishing she could get a hold of her feelings as readily.

'Who are you?' Rose demanded, edgy at having an uninvited guest on her land.

Nate looked to Eve, his sparkling blues narrowing. 'I take it your sister didn't tell you I was coming.'

Eve's hackles rose with her chin. 'I told you I'd check and get back to you.'

'And when you didn't, I figured no news, no objection.'

Rose looked between them, Opal tossing her head as though sensing her rider's confusion. 'Would one of you care to explain?'

'Rose, this is Nate.'

'Nate Harrington,' the man himself said. Dismounting and offering a hand up to Rose.

'George's son?'

'The very same.'

Rose shook his hand with continued reservation. 'And you're here because…?'

'Your sister suggested that it might benefit your cause if I were to see you in action, spend a day in your shadow, so to speak.'

Rose snapped back upright. 'Eve suggested *what*?'

She looked to her and Eve could do nothing but shrug. Her throat was too tight, her stomach rolled like a revolving door, and she feared if she opened her mouth anything could come out.

'Hell, I don't have time for this. If you're shadowing us, you can make yourself useful. You ever mustered before?'

'I got involved with my fair share of competitions in my teens.'

Rose's lips quirked. 'Still ride?' She eyed his bike. 'A horse, that is.'

'It's been a while but—'

'Good. Get a horse. Get a hat.' She turned to Eve. 'And *you* can explain later. Make sure he has all he needs. You can catch us up in the paddocks.'

She urged Opal into a canter and Nate watched her go, a slant to his smile. 'Is your sister always so...welcoming?'

'If you'd *been* welcome, yes.'

He gave her the side eye and her belly danced. 'Are you saying I'm not welcome, Eve?'

'I'm saying you should have waited.'

'I waited plenty. And I had a sneaking suspicion I'd be six feet under if I carried on wating for you to come to me.' He faced her fully now, those blazing blue eyes sending her weak at the knees—thank heaven for Jade beneath her. 'It may surprise you to know but I'm not one for sitting back and letting someone else take the lead. Not even when that someone is as sexy as you.'

Her heart gave a betraying little leap, Jade gave a whinny, and she pulled on the reins, dismissing his words as swiftly as she dismissed the way he made her feel. 'This way.'

She urged Jade into a canter, uncaring that he couldn't keep pace. She needed the space, a moment to recover. A moment to get over the shock of having him here when she was still reeling from the shock she had yet to share.

News she didn't know how to deliver.

Though she had to.

Secrets had crippled her family and she wasn't about to let this secret do the same. Not that they were family, but then…

Her stomach lurched and she pulled back on the reins, slowing Jade as she touched a hand to the invisible life growing inside her. *We're family.*

She'd never envisaged this in her future, but she wouldn't fail her child. And she wouldn't keep their presence from their father either. She'd tell him as soon as the day was done. As soon as Rose had received the help she needed.

And then she might start coming to terms with it herself.

No sooner had Nate entered the stables than Eve was shoving an Akubra at his chest.

'This isn't some joke, you know.'

'I didn't say it was.'

'Then quit with the grinning and stick this on. I'd lose the jacket else you'll cook. You got a decent shirt on under that?'

She waved a hand over him, but not once did her eyes reach his.

'I'll be fine.'

'And don't expect Rose to go easy on you. *Ev*eryone pulls their weight on the muster.'

'I wouldn't have it any other way.'

'Good.'

She gave an abrupt nod and started to move away. He caught at her arm, forcing her to pause and the pulse in her throat gave a betraying leap. He was getting to her. He just wasn't sure why… unless…

'I'm sorry if I overstepped.' It was the only reason he could think to explain her behaviour. The way she couldn't even look at him. 'The sexy remark, I mean.'

Not for the turning up unannounced, because she'd had her warning there.

She wet her lips, her eyes slowly lifting to his. 'It would help if you—'

'Here you go, Eve. Mercury was saddled for Aaron, but he's taking the Jeep so…' A tall brunette woman led an *extremely* tall black horse towards them. Glossy coat. Warm eyes. But how tall!

Nate had a flash of sanity. The last time he'd got on a horse had been…well, too many years ago to recall. Still, it had to be like riding a bike. Surely. He hoped.

'Thanks, Sally.'

Eve took the reins and handed them over, mouth twitching. 'I'm sure you'll be very happy together.'

She knew he was nervous!

Standing taller, he perfected his grin. 'Jealous?'

Her eyes flashed. There was something she wanted to say but she was biting her lip, and he knew better than to ask with an audience.

'Shall we get to work?' he said, tossing his jacket on a nearby barrel.

Her brow puckered, tease shifting into genuine concern. 'Are you sure about this?'

So she did care…or was it more that she didn't want an injured lawyer on her hands? On Rose's hands?

'Mustering? I wouldn't do it if I wasn't.' He turned to Mercury, gave the fine animal an affectionate stroke, which he returned with a nuzzle to his shirt. 'See, already one. Now lead the way before your sister accuses me of keeping you too long.'

That got her moving.

And watching Eve launch herself into the saddle and ride with effortless ease was as captivating as watching her walk. He followed suit, slightly less graceful but he had Mercury trotting and that was a start. Though he was more than aware of the barely constrained power between his thighs and was careful to respect it. Riding was as much about the mental and emotional awareness as it was the physical. He remembered that well enough.

They joined Rose and the stable hands in the field. Rose gave him a brief nod and the others followed suit. No one looked surprised so she must have filled them in.

'You okay?' Eve called over. Skin and hair golden with the rising sun, she made quite the sight and he almost lost his seat.

'Never better,' he called back, giving Mercury an apologetic pat for his ineptness while covering up his slip.

She gave a laugh. 'I'll ask you again in a few

hours when that bum of yours is protesting the saddle.'

She clicked her horse and moved off, reintroducing the distance she'd created when he'd first arrived and this time, he let her go. There would be time for them to talk later.

Right now, he'd enjoy the view. The mountains in the distance and nature all around—this was what he'd come back for. Sydney was still beautiful in its own way, but nothing could beat this.

Especially when a certain blonde woman and her bay took centre stage.

'Who'd have thought it?'

Rose came up alongside her, her eyes on Nate in the distance as he rounded up two escapees.

'Thought what?' Eve said, doing her best *not* to look his way. He was too much of a distraction. Had been all morning. Not because he wasn't capable. Because he was the exact opposite.

'The pretty boy can muster.'

Eve gave a choked laugh. 'I guess he can.'

'Works hard too.'

'He was a top lawyer in Sydney. I think he knows how to work hard.'

'With those tattoos?'

He'd rolled his cuffs back just enough to give them away...

'I don't think his tattoos affect his ability to work, Rose.'

'That's not what I meant, more the being a law-yer with all that ink…'

'Uh-huh.' Maybe that was why Eve had never guessed at his identity that first night, prejudiced from the outset…

'But this kind of graft is a different beast entirely.'

'Uh-huh,' she repeated, trying to dull her body's innate response to him that was increasing with every passing remark. Even though her sister was only saying everything she'd already thought. Her admiration increasing with every passing muster minute.

Rose gave her an odd look, which Eve promptly ignored.

'Right, we're going to stop for lunch,' her sister said, nodding to the river ahead. 'Let the cattle get some water. I need to catch up with Aaron on the satellite phone. You okay taking care of…?'

Rose's eyes were back on Nate and Eve swallowed. 'No problem.'

Only of course it was, because the secret was pressing between them, as was the incessant chemistry.

She urged Jade into a trot and, as though sensing her approach, Nate turned in his saddle, eyes bright beneath the rim of his Akubra, and her heart fluttered. Would there ever come a time he wouldn't do that to her?

'We're going to stop for lunch,' she said once he was within earshot. 'There's a shaded spot at the edge of the ravine. We can keep an eye on the cattle from there.'

'Right you are, Boss.'

His voice too, it got to her in all the ways she shouldn't let it but couldn't prevent.

And his unwitting use of Rose's nickname almost had her rejecting it out of hand. But it felt good. Earning that respectful title in the paddocks. Something she'd craved for so long. Even if he hadn't meant it in the same way they all did when they spoke to Rose.

She found a spot to secure the horses and threw a blanket over a nearby rock. Taking the food and water from the cooler pack, she set it all out. Ignored the sense that this was far too cosy and focused on the sticky heat and sweat of hard labour. Nothing sexy about that.

She plonked herself down and he lowered himself beside her.

'Here.'

Blindly, she offered him a sandwich, which he took with a gruff, 'Thank you.'

She heard him chug down some water, felt the heat of him relax back beside her as she took in the view. The craggy ravine to one side with the river running through it and the open red land to the other, the sparse pockets of green and the sun beating down. The cattle and the horses happily making the most of the water. The station hands finding a spot to settle for a spell...though she felt anything but settled.

She picked up her drink, took a swig, wishing it could chill her out too…

'You've impressed Rose,' she said, needing to say something to break the silence that was loaded with so much—the pull, the secret…

'Not you though?'

She could hear the tease in his voice and felt her lips curve. 'All right, don't get a big head about it. You've impressed us both.'

'I must be doing something right if you're back to dishing out compliments.'

She shook her head as she recalled that first night. It felt so long ago and yet it was only a month. So much had changed. She had changed. *Everything* had changed.

'To be honest,' he said, 'it's good to do something physical for a change.'

Physical. Not the evocative word she needed right now. 'Well, you're good at it.'

'So are you.' He took a bite of his sandwich as her body bloomed with his praise. 'Seems us office types can still pull it out of the bag when required.'

She gave a huffed laugh. 'I guess we can.'

And did that mean he'd been in awe of her all morning, as she had been in awe him? She'd sensed his eyes on her often enough but each time she'd checked him out his attention had been on the cattle…busy doing the job she was supposed to be doing.

'It is beautiful here,' he murmured while she picked at the sandwich she'd taken up.

'It is.'

He gave a chuckle that jarred her into looking at him. A foolish move. With him this close and laid back, propped up on one elbow, legs outstretched, the hat, those tattoos, the sheen of hard work...*why* was that sexy?

She tugged her gaze away. 'What's so funny?'

'After your whole speech in the bar I expected you to tell me how horrid it all was.'

'I never said it was horrid.'

Though all those weeks ago he was right...but now...

'No.' He took another bite of his sandwich, swallowed it with relish. 'You only gave that impression with the whole dreading-it thing and wishing for escape.'

She drank more water. Waited for her pulse to calm. Her nausea to ease.

'I love London. I love my life there.' All things she was trying to convince herself of as she said them because how could that change within a month? Because of Nate, Rose, her family...or the baby? Sure, it blurred things, shifted her priorities, but she still loved what she had back home. Didn't she? 'It gave me everything I needed when I left Australia.'

'Which was?'

'The aforementioned escape.'

'From?'

Like he didn't already know...but then she hadn't

told him the full story. She shoved her sandwich aside and brought her knees to her chest.

'I found out about the affair when I was fifteen and it broke me. It broke my life. I couldn't bear being under the same roof as my father…or my mother. I also couldn't bear being around my sisters knowing what I knew.'

'You never told them?'

'How could I? It was bad enough that I knew. I couldn't destroy their happy bubble too. They found out the day your father read Holt's will.'

He cursed under his breath.

'Precisely. I stopped coming home from boarding school in the holidays and left for England as soon as I was able. My grandparents took me in. Gave me all the love I could have wished for. I guess I filled the hole my mother left when she married my father and, though I never told them what my father did, their resentment towards him was enough to reaffirm how I felt. That I was better off out of it.'

'Did they really not speak to your mother after she married him…? Sorry, I'm not one to listen to gossip but it's hard to avoid that story.'

She picked at some muck on her boot. 'I know the stories, but my grandparents were good people. They loved Mum and they missed her terribly. They resented Holt for taking her away. They didn't trust him to do right by her and they didn't trust the intense passion they shared. Time proved them right.'

'Did it?'

'He had the affair, didn't he?'

'But then they had all those years…?'

'Doesn't change the heartache in between.'

'But if they hadn't cut her off, maybe your mother wouldn't have felt so isolated and—'

'And there you go again, sounding just like Rose.'

'She thinks the same?'

Eve nodded.

'But not you?'

'I don't know what to think. But I do know they regret it. My grandfather died a few years back and he told my grandmother to fix it.'

'Fix it?'

'To heal the rift. I love my grandmother and I love my sisters. To see them come together after all this time would be…'

'Would be wonderful, for sure.' He finished for her. 'But if your grandmother deserves a second chance, don't you think your father…?'

She glared at him.

'Seriously, Eve, think about it… How do your sisters feel now they know the truth?'

She went back to the muck on her boot. 'They loved my father, still love him, but it's different for them.'

'How is it different?'

They'd read her mother's journal, for a start.

'Eve?'

'They're convinced there is another side to all of this and one that I'd get if I just—'

She broke off as she thought of the aged leather book on her bedside table. It had turned up when she'd been in the shower one day courtesy of Rose and her unwavering hope that she would one day have the courage…

'Just?'

She swallowed. 'If I read my mother's journal.'

'Your mother kept a journal?'

'Her doctor recommended she keep one, when she was sick… She had PND—postnatal depression—after having Tilly. She was to use it as a way of pouring her feelings onto paper, a kind of therapy, I suppose.'

'And your sisters have read it, but you haven't?'

'No.' She shivered and clutched her knees tight. 'It feels like an invasion of privacy. Too personal and too wretched.'

'But she was your Mum.'

'I know, and Rose and Tilly think she meant for us to read it one day… A way of her explaining the past in a way that we as adults would understand, but…'

'That sounds reasonable.'

'I'm glad you all think so because it gives me the willies.'

He chuckled softly. 'Not a phrase I've heard in a long time.'

She managed a smile.

'Willies aside, it could be a way for you to get some closure on the past. Answers to all those questions you still have?'

She looked at him. 'You really do sound like Rose, you know?'

'Having witnessed your sister in action this morning, I'm going to take that as another compliment.'

'You would.'

'I'm also going to say that, for someone who professes to love London, you do look rather at home here.'

'It seems it's in my blood more than I thought, but I struggle to understand how you can give up your life, your work in Sydney, to come back for good.'

'Like you, I left as soon as I could. I didn't want to stew in my own anger and resentment and make things worse for Mum. I figured getting away made it easier. My father couldn't overlook me any more, because I wasn't here to be overlooked.'

She lowered her knees and twisted to face him. 'Have you spoken to him yet?'

'No.'

'But now that you know more about the past, about him, don't you think you owe it to you both to clear the air? He's not a bad man. He's made mistakes. And I know I sound like a hypocrite...'

'You do.'

'But what if he doesn't realise that's how you felt growing up? What if—?'

'Doesn't change the fact that it happened.'

'And yet, you want to make a life for yourself here now.'

'I told you, it's where I want to settle, where I've

always intended to settle. Sydney gave me the career to build up a nest egg that, with the right investment, I don't need to work the hours that I did in the city. I'm in a place where I can take time out. I can even help the people of Marni like my father did before and still have a life, marry, make a home.'

Marry. Make a home. *Children.*

She covered her stomach with her palm, the truth rising within her. 'Nate, I—'

A whistle pierced the air. They both turned to see Rose gesturing.

'Lunch over already?' he asked.

She nodded. As was the time to talk. Not that now had been the time or the place for it…

'We need to keep moving if we're to make it back before nightfall.'

Then she could talk to him. Alone. No distractions.

No more secrets.

To say Nate struggled to focus for the remainder of the day was an understatement.

Eve was a distraction like none other.

Majestic on her bay, forthright with the cattle, the rhythmic sounds coming out of her throat enough to make him want to dance to her tune.

Regardless of what he'd told her that morning…

'I'm not one for sitting back and letting someone else take the lead. Not even when that someone is as sexy as you.'

He'd hardly been playing it cool. The words coming out of his mouth before he could wind them back in. And she'd fled from him. No sooner had the spark come alive in her blue eyes, than it had been snuffed out and she'd ridden off. He was beginning to spy a pattern. Any time he evoked anything close to the passion they'd shared that first night, she ran.

And he got it.

She feared it because she didn't trust it. She didn't trust it to last and not bite you on the arse when it was done.

But it existed. Between them. And damned if he could snuff it out.

The attraction, the chemistry, the inability to get her out of his head. The admiration that ran far deeper than attraction. The last few weeks she'd dedicated herself to Garrison Downs and her sisters' cause, whether it was pulling apart the will or physically working herself to the bone to keep the station ticking over. It all pointed to her huge heart that she refused to give to anyone else. And what a crime that was.

He'd tell her as much if he didn't think it would send her even faster in the other direction. His eyes drifted back to her, prepared for more of the same—appreciation, admiration, desire...instead his senses came alive with concern. Her pace had slowed, her head lolling with the movement of her horse, her posture slackening...

He looked to Rose, alert in her seat, no sign of

tiredness. But then, Rose lived and breathed this life. Eve was like him. Unaccustomed to such labour. He'd been at it a day and he was dog tired, but he knew Eve had been at it for days, weeks even, and something wasn't right.

She wasn't right.

He stiffened and Mercury whinnied in response, the horse jerking towards Eve as his body instinctually did the same.

'Sorry, boy.'

He adjusted his seat, patted the horse's neck, all the while keeping his gaze trained on her. He wanted to get to her. Wanted to check on her. It was far enough to fall when you came off a horse, but with the driving cattle, too…it didn't bear thinking about.

He scanned the area, the station hands all spread out. They were thin enough on the ground as it was, he couldn't break formation. To get to Rose and warn her. Or get himself to Eve's side.

He cursed, wishing their pace to quicken even as he wished her off that horse and in his arms. Safe. He edged as close as he could without confusing the cattle and gritted his teeth. Held steady. Denying the impulse to speed up when the homestead appeared on the horizon, a tiny speck but a welcome sight.

Sweat trickled down his rigid spine, the tension nothing to do with the muster and everything to do with Eve. Though she seemed to perk up as they neared the house. Her posture returning, the odd smile too.

Maybe he'd been projecting his weariness onto her, worrying unnecessarily…

'And that's a wrap!' Rose called out as the gate was swung shut on the last of the cattle. 'Great job, guys. Rest up, catch your beauty sleep. It's going to be a big day tomorrow.'

Then she turned to Nate. 'Toss your reins to Kylie and she'll see Mercury back to the stables. Thanks for your help today.'

'My pleasure.'

He sought out Eve, surprised to find her still mounted on Jade and walking steadily away. Then he took in her hands slack on the reins, her head starting to droop…

'*Eve!*'

He dropped Mercury's reins and ran, catching the attention of the entire yard. Rose's head and horse snapped around. But his every sense was on Eve. Desperate, unable to breathe, praying her horse wouldn't startle as he came up alongside her. He reached a hand up to steady her as he slowed Jade to a stop and Eve slumped towards him, silent, unmoving.

His heart lurched. 'Eve…?'

He eased her into his arms, stroked the hair away from her face. Took in the pulse working in her throat—reassuring. The paleness to her skin—less so.

He cursed and her head lifted, her lashes fluttering open for the briefest spell. 'You kiss your momma with that mouth?'

Hell, he wanted to kiss her just for saying it. For giving him some fire.

'Evie!' Opal skidded to a halt in a cloud of dust and Rose swung herself down.

'It's okay. I've got her. I've got her.' His words were for Rose but his tone, soft and soothing, was all for Eve.

'How did you…?' Whatever Rose saw in his face stopped her from finishing. 'I should have noticed.' She cursed, snatching Eve's fallen Akubra off the ground. 'Aaron!' she yelled towards the bunkhouse as a guy appeared in the doorway. 'Get these horses back to the stables. Eve's taken ill.'

The chap jogged up to take the reins and Rose led Nate to the house. The second they crossed the threshold, she was hollering, 'Lindy! Lindy!'

A short brunette woman came running up, an old border collie trailing behind. 'What is it?' Her eyes widened on Eve in Nate's arms. 'Oh, my!'

'Get me a bowl of fresh water and a cloth,' Rose commanded. 'Iced water to drink and some food. Some soup. Eve's unwell.'

'I'm fine,' Eve murmured, her body still slack against him, her voice otherworldly.

'Like hell you are.' Rose spun to face them. Blue eyes, so like her sister's, ablaze. 'I *knew* there was something wrong with you this morning, I never should've let you work.' She tugged off her hat, ran a hand over her hair. 'You've likely caught what they've all had.'

'This isn't on you.' Eve shifted against him, tried to lift her head. 'It's not your fault.'

'Like hell it isn't.'

He could see the anger in Rose, anger that she lay wholly at her own feet.

'It really isn't, Rose,' he said softly, trying to re-assure her, for her own sake as well as Eve's. Rose's self-loathing was only going to exacerbate Eve's condition. 'You have a station to run and you were doing it.'

She blew out a shallow breath, muttered something that sounded an awful lot like *'But at what cost?'* and turned away. 'Follow me.'

He did as she asked, barely aware of the grand surroundings and the dirt they were traipsing through as she led him down the hallway to a door towards the end. She pushed it open and strode on in, switching on a bedside lamp and throwing back the duvet. The dog came too, alert to something amiss as it took up position at the foot of the bed.

Everything was pink—the walls, the bed, the chair before the window... Was this Eve's bed-room? Was this how she'd had it as a child? All sweet and romantic and soft?

He set her down gently and Rose tugged off her sister's boots, still tutting and muttering. Nate set his hat down on the bedside table and stroked her cheeks, felt her forehead for a temperature. They were inches apart, so close he could catch her unique scent, feel her breath upon his skin. Her blue eyes blinked up at him, her gaze far off and smile meek. 'My hero.'

Unadulterated pleasure morphed into white-hot panic as her lashes fluttered closed again and she sank back into the pillow. He lurched forward, tapped her cheek. '*Eve?* Eve, stay with me.'

'I'm fine.' She tried to bat his hands away. 'I'm just—just tired.'

Lindy came in with a bowl, her frown deep. 'Aaron needs to see you, Rose. He says it's urgent.'

'Right now? I can't—'

'Don't worry, Rose,' Nate said, taking the bowl from Lindy. 'I'll take care of your sister. You do what you need to.'

A small crease formed between her brows. A moment where she studied him intently, then gave a sharp nod. He had the oddest sense that he'd just been read, tested, and given some kind of approval.

'I'll be right back.'

'You don't need to do this,' Eve mumbled as Rose left and he shushed her as he eased himself down beside her, wringing the cloth in the water.

'I want to.'

Gently, he mopped her brow, her cheeks, her neck, cleaning her skin while cooling her down. Always careful, always aware of her every reaction. The flicker of her lashes, the reassuring rise and fall of her chest, the way she turned into his touch...

Lindy came in and placed a jug of water and a

glass beside the bed. He nodded his gratitude, and she hurried off again.

'You can go now,' she whispered.

'Always so keen to get rid of me, Eve.'

Her lips quivered into a small smile. 'You've served your purpose.'

'Thought you said I was your hero.'

'For saving me from a nasty fall…'

He dabbed at her temple. 'I think a hero would stick around, don't you?'

She gave a soft laugh. 'Don't be getting a big head.'

He recalled her saying the same at the ravine, when she'd told him how impressed she'd been, and he smiled. 'I wouldn't dare.'

'Though I wish mine would stop banging.'

'You have a headache?'

She nodded and winced in one.

He scanned the room, spied the door to her en suite. 'Don't go anywhere…'

'Fat chance,' she said softly.

He headed into the bathroom—just as pink, just as girly—pulled open the bathroom cabinet and found a blister pack of paracetamol.

'I have tablets,' he said, returning to her side. 'Do you feel up to taking them?'

She scooted herself up the bed in answer and he poured a glass of water.

'I've really made a fool of myself,' she grumbled, eyeing him from beneath her lashes, the colour in her cheeks deepening.

'What you've done is worked too hard and your body needs a break.'

He popped out the last two tablets in the pack and offered them out with the glass.

She threw them back with a sip of water and screwed up her face. 'So much for proving we can run this place.'

He took the glass from her as she sagged back into the pillow.

'Really messed that up, didn't I?'

'You didn't mess it up at all. Seeing you Waverly sisters in action was quite something.'

'Quite something…in a *good* way?'

'Yes, Eve, in a very good way.'

Her eyes lifted to his. Surprise, doubt, gratitude, a swirling mist within the blue and he had to look away. Look away before the connection brewing got the better of him. He placed her glass back on the bedside table and saw the leather-bound book resting there. Aged and initialled with RW. 'Is that…?'

She followed his gaze. 'Yes.' She swallowed. 'Rose is ever hopeful I'll pick it up.'

'Does she not know how stubborn you are?'

She gave a soft laugh that was music to his still-worry-spiked pulse. 'Jokes aside, maybe it's time, Eve. Maybe it's time we both dealt with our parents head-on. You with your mother's written word and me with my father.'

'Are you offering some sort of a deal?'

'Perhaps.' He let his gaze drift back to hers, saw

the hair that had fallen across one eye and tucked it back behind her ear. 'But maybe not tonight, hey? Tonight, you need to rest.'

She raised her hand to cover his, held his palm against her cheek. 'Thank you.'

'What for?'

Her blue eyes glistened and she wet her lips…

'Eve?'

But no words came. The room was so quiet save for their gentle breaths, the light so soft it felt as intimate as any embrace. He had the strangest sense of being where he belonged, of being beside the woman he belonged to…

It didn't matter that she wasn't the woman for him, that under any normal circumstances she was married to her job just as his father had always been, that she had no interest in marriage, kids, a family of her own.

He wanted her to be the right woman because she was everything he wanted.

'How's the patient?'

His head flicked around as Rose stepped into the room.

'Sorry, I didn't mean to startle you.'

'You didn't, I was…' What were you doing? Fantasising about a future that wasn't possible, with a woman who wouldn't want it in a million years. Because this wasn't *Eve* Eve. This was Eve on sabbatical, exhausted and strung out.

'I've asked Lindy to make up one of the guest rooms for you,' Rose said, rescuing him from his runaway thoughts as she checked Eve over. 'It's too late to be travelling back now and it's the least we can do for all your help today. Not to mention rescuing Bambi here.'

He cocked a brow. 'Bambi?'

'Rose,' Eve moaned. 'Do you have to?'

'Sorry, little sis,' she said softly, 'couldn't resist.'

'You don't need to know,' Eve mumbled, reaching for his hand and squeezing it.

'Need, no.' He covered her hand around his. 'But *want*? Definitely.'

She growled.

'Eve can explain it to you tomorrow,' Rose said. 'For now, I can take it from here.'

He wanted to argue. Say he was happy to stay. But Rose was her sister, and he…well, he was nobody by comparison.

Reluctantly, he stood.

'There's nothing to take, Rose,' Eve said. 'I'm fine.'

'You will be when you get some soup in you and a decent night's sleep.'

'All things I can do by myself.'

Snatching up the empty strip of pills, Nate headed to the bathroom, listening to Rose fuss and Eve deflect, warmed by the sisterly to and fro. All signs that Eve would be okay.

He flicked up the lid of the pedal bin and tossed the strip in. A good night's sleep and she'd be—

He froze. Eyes on the contents of the bin as the world spun around him. There, lay the empty blis-

ter pack. And beneath it, a tiny mountain of tests—
Pregnancy tests.

All with their own version of the same result:

Pregnant
Positive
+

Eve was...*pregnant*?

Dazed and confused, his eyes drifted to her on
the bed. Rose, in the position he'd vacated...

This room was Eve's. This bathroom was Eve's.
Those tests *had* to be Eve's.

She chose that moment to look in his direction,
their eyes connecting, hers falling to his foot still
on the pedal bin before launching back to his face,
panicked and wide.

He knew in that moment. The baby was his.

She started to push herself up.

'Oh, no, you don't.' Rose pressed her back.

'But, Rose...'

Nate moved before all hell broke loose, heading
for the door as everything within him went into
full-on turmoil. Every emotion at war. 'Thank you
for the offer of a bed, Rose. I'll see you both in the
morning. We'll talk then, Eve.'

When she was rested and he was dealing with
her at full strength. Because there could be no confusion where their baby was concerned. Where the
future was concerned.

The idea that she would simply return to London and take their child with her…that he would become worse than his father, a true absentee dad, access restricted by the miles and granted as and when life permitted. *Hell*, no.

Eve might have proven that Holt Waverly's daughters didn't need husbands to run these lands, but, as the mother of his child, she *would* marry him.

CHAPTER EIGHT

'NATE!'

Eve woke with a start, Nate's face as he'd connected the dots the night before injecting her with adrenaline and sending her bolt upright in bed. Hand clutched to her chest, she sucked in a breath and another, her heart beating so hard she was sure she'd break a rib.

'Good. You're awake…'

She turned at the sound of his voice, her heart struggling to return to its normal rhythm. Immaculate in the clothes from yesterday—dark shirt open at the collar, blue jeans, buckle belt and blond hair styled to perfection—he was everything her panicked heart wanted to see and not.

'You look…fresh.' She'd hoped to coax out a smile as he crossed the room, instead she got a cool aloofness that had the hairs prickling along her bare arms. She hugged the quilt to her chest, lowered her gaze from his eyes that seemed to look right past her. 'I take it Lindy managed to clean your clothes.'

'Rose insisted.' He paused beside the bed, pressed

a gentle hand to her brow. His touch warm but his voice... 'How are you feeling?'

'Better.' But it came out gruff, fearful, choked with the mood in the room. She glanced up. Took in the shadows under his eyes, his mouth...*that* mouth, normally so quick to smile, drawn into a pensive line.

She'd done that to him. Worried him. Shocked him. Made him into this cool replica of himself...

'Where's Rose?' Was that really her voice? So quiet and unsure.

'You've been asleep a while. She left shortly after the doctor arrived.'

'Doctor? What doctor?'

'He helicoptered in from Marni this morning. His assurances that you weren't in any immediate danger are the only reason Rose isn't here now watching over you.'

'Oh, my God, does she know?'

He backed away, his 'No' short. 'I surmised she had no idea about—about the situation.'

Situation. That was one word for it.

And the feeling of guilt welled with the panic.

Guilt that she was adding to her sister's burden. Guilt that Nate knew but not from her lips. And panic that she'd lost any grip on the situation as the man before her pulled away. Emotionally as well as physically.

Where was the connection they'd shared not twenty-four hours ago? The man who had nursed her, cared for her...made her feel safe and invincible?

He paused before the window, his back to her, rigid and unmoving. Did he even breathe?

'I'm sorry.'

He didn't flinch, there was no sign he'd even heard her.

'I hate that you found out like that.'

She wrapped her arms around her knees and her rapidly chilling middle. Watched as he turned his head, just enough for her to see his profile, the grim set of his mouth, his eyes downcast. 'How long have you known?'

She clenched her teeth and swallowed. This wasn't how she wanted this to go, wasn't how she'd expected it to go. But then, she hadn't really known *what* to expect. She knew what she craved though. Some of his usual warmth, his charisma, his care...

'I suspected a couple of days ago.'

Slowly he turned to face her. 'Why didn't you say anything when I saw you in town?'

'Because I didn't know. Not for certain. That's why I was there.'

'The pharmacy—that's what you were doing?'

'Buying them out of every brand of test, yes. I took them yesterday morning. They say it's best, more accurate, if you do it then.'

She threw back the covers, making to rise, and he was before her in a heartbeat. 'Oh, no, you don't, you're staying there.'

'I'm pregnant, Nate! Not debilitated.' They both

froze at her declaration, and it was Nate who recovered first. Taking a step back.

'I'd appreciate you staying there until the doctor has spoken to you. There are tests he needs to carry out.'

'I don't need a doctor.'

'You fainted, Eve, multiple times.'

'I just needed sleep and some food. I feel fine.'

She didn't but she wasn't about to tell him that. She didn't want his pity. She *did* want him to wrap his arms around her and show her that he still cared though.

He surprised her with a curse. 'You should've said something sooner! If I'd known I'd never have let you…'

'What, ride? Help Rose? You really think you could have stopped me?'

'But it's not just you you need to think of now, Eve! There's our baby to consider.'

'And don't you think I know *that*? I may not have planned to be a mother, I may not have experienced the whole ticking of the biological clock, but I tell you now, I'll be a good one. I'll make sure of it.'

'I don't doubt it, but we need to talk about what we do now.'

'What we do?' She frowned. 'There'll be appointments, for sure. I haven't sorted anything as yet, but I guess with the doctor here…' Her voice trailed off at the look in his eye. 'That's not what you meant, is it?'

'No. Though we do need to talk about your prenatal care. You won't want for anything, you or my child. I can promise you that.'

And it should have warmed her, the passion in that statement, only...

'So if you didn't mean that, what did you mean?'

'I want to talk about us.'

'Us?'

'Yes.'

She frowned, shook her head. 'I'm not sure I follow...'

'You've made it clear that love is an emotion you will never fall foul of...that you don't want it in return and have no desire for it in your future.'

'Yes,' she whispered, even as her heart called her out for a fool and a liar. 'Though I'll love our child, Nate, don't doubt that.'

'I don't.'

'So what are you—?'

'Marry me, Eve.'

Her breath caught in her lungs, her eyes burning as she stared at him. He couldn't have just said... 'What?'

'Hear me out, okay?'

'Hear you out,' she repeated numbly, shock fixing her in place.

'I refuse to be like my father. You already know this about me. I won't bring a child up wondering when they'll next see me, when the next scrap of affection will be tossed their way. I wanted for nothing financially growing up, but emotionally...' He swallowed. 'I won't do it. I can't.'

'But *marriage*?'

'I want to be there every day, not just at weekends or when our schedules permit it. I want a home, with a wife and our child.'

'But, Nate…' She was shaking, from her toes to the tips of her fingers. 'You can't mean it.'

'I do. You need a husband to satisfy the conditions of the will and I refuse to let another man bring up my child, Eve. I want you to marry me. I'm *asking* you to marry me.'

'You don't know what you're saying.'

'I know exactly what I'm saying.'

'But you want love, Nate, you *deserve* love.'

'What I want is your hand in marriage. What I deserve is a home where I see my child every day.'

Her ears rang, her heart raced.

'I know you don't want love, Eve, and I'll respect that, if you will respect my wishes in return.'

She studied his face, searched for the man she had come to care for so deeply…

'But where will we live? Have you thought about that? My life is in London, my job, Gran…the idea that I would leave her like Mum once left her…'

'You won't have to.'

'But—?'

'We'll move to London.'

'You're going to come to London? With *me*?'

'I'll move anywhere to be there for my child, so long as it's a place that can give them what they need.'

She swallowed. 'But London?'

He nodded.

'I can't believe you're serious.'

'Why can't you? It works for you too. This way, you secure your part in the inheritance and can return to London with a free conscience. Go back to your job, your life.'

Ha. Her life was unrecognisable now. Couldn't he see that?

'And you, what will you do there?'

'I can be a lawyer anywhere.'

'But what about continuing your father's good work in Marni?'

'I'm sure London has its fair share of people in need of legal aid.'

'But what about your love of the land here, the home and the life you wanted for your child?'

'We can do all that in London.'

'In the city? That is as busy and as bustling as Sydney?'

'I'm sure there'll be quieter suburbs, somewhere we can both be happy.'

Happy. It didn't sound happy to Eve. It sounded cold and lonely and…and…she couldn't bear it.

'What about when I'm working and my job takes over once more? When I'm no better than your father for the time I'll have spare?'

He shifted on his feet, not quite so quick. 'I'll deal with it. I'm not a teen craving attention any more, Eve.'

No, he was a man craving love. The kind she didn't trust and sure as hell didn't know how to give.

'You don't need to decide this second. I've told Rose I'll stay on for a few days and help with the muster.'

'*I* should be out there helping.'

'You're going nowhere.'

'But, Nate, it's the busiest time of the year. She needs me.'

'What she needs is her sister and the niece or nephew she doesn't know exists healthy. The doctor will decide if and when you're ready to help again.'

She blinked at him, speechless. How had it come to this? How had she become such an epic burden to her sister who she'd come here to help? And this man who deserved so much more than she felt capable of giving?

'In the meantime, I'm here to take your place so you needn't worry about Rose and the station.'

'And what about your work?'

'You and my child come first, Eve.'

Something else she'd always known about him… so why did it still leave her cold?

'I'm going to let the doctor know you're awake.'

He moved and she shot up. 'Nate, wait—'

He paused, looked back, but she couldn't find the words. None that made sense anyhow. Because all she really wanted was for him to hold her. Hold her and make her feel as though everything would be okay. Just like he had that first night.

But she wasn't so sure that was possible…or if it ever would be again.

As for the offer he'd put to her...marriage, the inheritance, their child.

Was there really any other answer she could give?

'Eve?'

'Yes,' she said over him.

He took a sharp breath. 'Yes?'

'I'll marry you.'

CHAPTER NINE

I<small>T WAS</small> F<small>RIDAY EVENING</small>.

Five days since she'd said yes. Six days with Nate under the same roof, helping Rose and the station. Helping her.

And still no one knew. Not about the engagement or her pregnancy.

Well, save for Nate and the doctor.

She hadn't wanted to distract Rose. Or so she'd told Nate. But really, she hadn't wanted to put words to it. It all felt too surreal.

Her. Pregnant and engaged.

She felt railroaded. Not by Nate. Never, Nate. But by the situation. The situation brought about by her father and the inheritance. And then the baby, the baby that she wanted to ensure would be brought up encased in love, from both their parents, and would never doubt that love. Not for a second.

It was like some parallel universe where she was doing the very opposite of every plan she'd made since hitting adulthood. Every dream.

She watched from the front deck as Rose and Nate rolled home with the troops. Signalling the end of a very long week and the start of a new life for Eve, because tonight was the night. Nate wanted to visit his folks, share the 'good' news, and she wanted to break it to Rose before they left.

Taking some nausea-easing breaths, she eased the swing seat beneath her back and forth. Waiting as they dismounted in the yard. Waiting as they crossed the ground towards her, laughing and joking as if Nate had always belonged here. Waiting until…his eyes met hers, her heart did its little dance, and she gave the half-smile she'd perfected in Rose's company of late.

'You look nice,' Rose said as she stepped up onto the deck, stripping her hat and sweeping a hand through her hair. 'It's good to see you looking more like yourself.'

'Thanks.' She only wished she felt like it. Her eyes flitted to Nate, seeking his approval too. She hadn't known what to wear and had settled on a blue button-up midi dress, covered in tiny roses, feminine and sweet. A light dusting of make-up, hair loose in styled waves, she'd even misted on some perfume…

Perfect fiancée material.

'You do,' he said with a hint of warmth, of appreciation, but it was quickly masked. Hidden by the cool facade. Something she was getting far too accustomed to seeing. So much so she questioned whether the glimpses were all in her hormonal imagination. 'My parents will love you.'

Love…?

'Your parents?' Rose frowned at Nate.

'Nate's taking me for dinner with them tonight.'

Rose cocked a brow. 'Is he now?'

Eve swallowed. 'Yes.'

He gave her a discreet nod. 'Which means I need to get moving if I'm to freshen up before we leave.'

Rose watched him go, her mouth quirking to one side. 'First, he rescues you from a fall he saw happening long before I did. Second, he helps nurse you back to health. Third, he has his receptionist bring clothes so that he can stick around to help our station get through the week. And *now* he's taking you to see his parents?'

Her gaze returned to Eve, blue eyes curious and questioning.

'Come and sit with me?'

She frowned, sensing something amiss, but did as Eve asked.

'Though I'm not coming any closer with this layer of muck. I'll ruin your dress.'

Eve managed a smile.

'So…you going to tell me what's going on between you both?'

Eve pressed her palms into her knees and took a breath. 'We're getting married.'

'You're *what*?'

Eve winced. 'Do you want all the dingoes to come running?'

'But you…you only met a month ago. How can you possibly be…? Is this the will? Because when I said I'd consider marrying, you were…'

Eve was shaking her head.

'Wow.' Rose tugged on her ponytail, looked to the sun setting over the land. 'I can't believe this. I knew there was more going on. I knew he cared for you. But *marriage*? So quick?'

'We've spent a lot of time together.'

Her sister gave her a disbelieving look.

'More than you know.'

The look stayed.

'So much time, we're actually… I'm…we're…'

Rose leaned closer. 'You're…'

Eve swallowed the rolling sickness within her. 'I'm pregnant.'

'Pregnant!'

Again, Eve winced and this time Rose apologised, leaned closer to give a hushed, '*Pregnant? And it's…?*'

Eve cursed. 'Yes, it's his!'

'Sorry.' Rose pinched her nose. 'I'm just…surprised. It's a lot to take in.'

'Tell me about it.'

'But when you first met, you were steaming angry.'

Eve coloured. 'That wasn't the first time we met…'

Rose's head lifted a nudge. 'It wasn't?'

Eve shook her head, wet her lips. 'We met in Marni the night I arrived… We hit it off.'

'Some hitting it off!'

The flicker of a smile touched Eve's lips. 'Bonded over Daddy issues, would you believe?'

'That old chestnut?'

Eve nodded. 'I can't explain it, Rose. There was just this *connection*. This intense, out-of-this-world connection. We didn't know who the other was, but we learned plenty, and we had this chemistry, and it was enough. We slept together. A lot.'

Rose gave an awkward laugh, held up a hand. 'Okay. TMI.'

'Sorry, but it was crazy,' she stressed. 'I've never known anything like it.'

'Me neither,' Rose said. 'But I'll tell you who has…'

'Don't go there. Please. That connection destroyed, Mum.'

'I was going to say Tilly but, yes, Mum too. And it didn't destroy her, Eve, you're wrong.'

'Am I?' she threw back, fired by her panic and confusion over Nate. 'Dad felt it too and look what he did to Mum when she needed him the most.'

She saw the pain in Rose's eyes, felt it as fresh and as real as her own.

'People aren't perfect, Evie. Not you, not me, not anyone. And if you carry on placing everyone on that same infallible pedestal you did Dad, you'll be disappointed for ever. If you accepted that we all make mistakes and learn from them, your life would be so much easier.'

But if she did that, if she accepted that her father did indeed love her mother, that they did indeed love one another, then she'd also have to accept that she'd cut them out of her life for nothing. She'd lost them for nothing. Sacrificed all those years when she could have been with them, with her sisters, all that time with her family that she could never get back.

'Please, sweetheart.' Rose pulled her in for a hug and Eve went willingly, uncaring of the dirt, needing her sister's love and warmth more. 'Read Mum's journal. Give yourself the opportunity to make peace with them.'

Eve eased out of her sister's hold, eyed her hands as she twisted them together in her lap and thought of the little leather book beside her bed.

'I'm a firm believer that everything happens for a reason.' Rose covered Eve's hands with one of her own. 'What happened with Mum. Dad. Now you… I've watched that man as he's watched over you, Evie, and there isn't anyone else in this world that I would trust more with your future happiness. Well, save for me, but I don't really count.'

She met her sister's earnest gaze, wishing with all her heart she could believe it.

A week ago, she might have. Before the news of the baby and everything had changed between them. When they'd had the chemistry, the connection, when he'd smiled at her in that way, teased her, endearingly tried to tackle her past with her, then she would have believed it.

But now he was so detached, so aloof. Aside from his concern for her well-being, but then she carried his child. He had a vested interest in her health.

'Are you ready, Eve?'

They both turned to see the man himself standing in the doorway. Hair damp from the shower, white shirt rolled back at the cuffs, jeans, boots, and a smile so reserved Eve thought she might cry on the spot. Something that was happening an awful lot lately.

Hormones. Just hormones.

She stood with a nod.

Rose clutched her hand, gave it a squeeze, her eyes sharp as she looked to Nate. 'Take care of my sister.'

'Always.'

'How did she take it?' Nate asked when he couldn't handle the silence in the truck any longer.

'She was shocked. Even more when I told her about the baby.'

No surprise there. *He* was still in shock.

'But I think…'

She fell silent and he glanced her way. This past week he'd witnessed a change in her, and it wasn't for the better. She was quiet. Reserved. Wary. The confident city swan was no more and he didn't know how to get her back. It was taking everything to keep his cool around her, to keep his feelings tightly locked away.

Maybe he should have given her longer, given her more time to adjust…

And the chance to change her mind?

His hands pulsed around the wheel, his voice tight with his thoughts. 'You think?'

She gave him a wry smile.

'She says that she believes everything happens for a reason.'

He frowned, trying to read between the lines. 'So she's *okay* about it?'

'If she wasn't, you'd know.'

'Now that I believe.' He gave a strained laugh. 'That woman is fierce when protecting her own.'

'She is…' Her voice trailed off, her gaze too. 'Not that I deserve such protection.'

He balked at her whispered remark. 'Why would you say that?'

'Why would you question it?'

He fought the urge to reach for her. 'Eve…'

'What, Nate?' she threw back at him, twisting in her seat. 'I abandoned her when I left all those years ago. I wasn't around when Mum died. I wasn't around when Dad died. She went through all that hell and I didn't come running to help her.'

'Because you shouldered a secret you thought would destroy her. You can't condemn yourself for that.'

'I can, because I should have told her.'

'But you didn't, and you can't change that. Your motives were pure even if you regret it now.' He flexed his grip around the wheel. 'Is that what all this has been? Weeks of hard labour, of sacrificing your life in London to come back and fight their corner…some kind of penance?'

She didn't respond but he knew he was right.

He should pull over. He should make her listen to him.

But where would that end? On a deserted road with the tensions running high between them, the undeniable chemistry he'd been suppressing for days, too.

He took a steadying breath. 'You abandoned your life in London to come back for her. You chose to face your past and the pain it so evidently brought you, to be here for your family now. You deserve all the care and the love in return.'

His voice grew husky, his feelings creeping too close to the surface…feelings that would help to convince his mother their engagement was real but freak Eve out. And for that he had to warn her…

'Look, Eve, I don't know how much you know about my parents.'

'Right now, I love them for getting you off the topic of me.'

And he couldn't agree more. They both needed the change up.

'I didn't spend any real time with your father when I was younger,' she said, sincerely now. 'The will reading was via video call and I've never met your mother. All I have to go on is what you've told me.'

He rolled his head on his shoulders, trying to ease the budding tension along his spine.

'They're quite…traditional. Especially when it comes to marriage. More so my mother. And with me being an only child, I think those values are magnified.'

'By values, what you're really saying is she wants you to marry for love?'

'Yes.' His mother most definitely. As for his father, heaven knew what George wanted but the fact that Eve was a Waverly would outshine all else.

'And you're telling me this because…?'

'Because I'd appreciate it if we could at least pretend.'

She didn't blanch, didn't flinch. She seemed calmer than he thought possible.

'Of course.' She stroked her stomach, a gesture he'd caught her doing numerous times and he wondered whether she was aware of it. Or if it was some innate response. He certainly wanted to do it. *All* the time. Hold her, hold *them*. 'What have you told them?'

'Not a lot.'

'What's not a lot?'

'That we've been dating and that I'm bringing you for dinner.'

'That's it?'

'That's it.'

'Okay,' she drawled as he pulled into his parents' drive and then she gasped.

'What is it?' His eyes shot to her, his pulse skipping over with worry for her and the baby.

But she was smiling, eyes wide as she took in his childhood home. The white picket fence that bordered his mother's flourishing garden, the love seat beneath the desert oak tree that had been there long before he'd been born. The potted plants that lined the steps up to the veranda where his mother's favourite swing seat had pride of place.

'It's like something out of a fairy tale, a gingerbread cottage... You grew up here?'

He nodded. 'My mother is an old romantic and my father had it built for her.' He turned to look at her, surprised to see the returning sadness in her eyes. 'What's wrong?'

'What is it about men building homes for their wives?'

He shrugged. 'Beats me.'

'And yet, you're offering the same. Offering to uproot your life here to build a home for us in London.'

'Your job is your first love.' No bitterness, just fact. 'You adore your grandmother. You adore your life in London. And you're desperate to get back to it. Have I missed anything?'

She stared at him, quiet and pale, and he feared he'd gone too far closing himself off. He softened his voice, held her gaze. 'Look, Eve, I know how you feel about your mother uprooting her life in London to move here for your father. I know you think that fed into her misery.' He reached out to cup her cheek, wishing he could absorb her sadness through his palm and bring back the joy. Joy that he was witnessing less and less since his proposal. 'Knowing all this, I could never, in all good conscience, expect you to go through the same. To risk the same. I won't. You came back to help your sisters and once you've done that, we can leave.'

'But, Nate—'

Movement from the house caught their attention, his mother appearing on the doorstep. She waved, her eyes bright and smile wide. He took a moment to wave then turned back to Eve, who'd shrunk into her seat. Hiding from his mother or hiding from the reality of their situation, he wasn't sure.

'All that I ask is that we visit. Often.'

'But are you sure?' she whispered. 'Maybe we should take more time to think—'

'We're about to make my mother's dreams come true, Eve. There really is nothing more to think about...'

Because thinking about it meant questioning everything.

And questioning everything would bring answers.

And those potential answers terrified him.

Eve was ushered into the Harrington abode with all the care and affection one would expect to receive as a long-lost family member. Not a virtual stranger.

However, George had made it clear that, despite her absence, her father had spoken of her so often, he felt as though he already knew her. And Sue-Ellen hadn't stopped smiling. Her gaze darting between Eve and Nate as if she couldn't believe her eyes but adored what she saw.

And there'd been no fall out between the two men. Yet.

They talked about her sisters, the station, Rose and the mustering. There'd been the unmissable pride in his father's voice when he'd praised his son for stepping in and helping with the staffing. She wondered if Nate had noticed it too.

She looked at him now, sitting beside her at the cosy dining room table, and took his hand in hers. 'I really don't know what we would have done without Nate this past week.'

His eyes darted to hers, a momentary flare and then he caught her cue. Smiled softly.

'Yes, well…' George cleared his throat as his mother beamed on. 'It was very good of you, son, very good indeed.'

Nate gave her the smallest of nods—*Are you ready for us to tell them?*

A nervous smile—*Yes.*

Nerves ran riot in her gut. The news had been a shock to Rose and she'd had time to see them together, was convinced of their feelings too. His parents had witnessed one meal.

He grinned and the butterflies within her took off.

'It was nothing…especially for my soon-to-be wife.'

Woah. Had he really just thrown it out there like that?

His mother gasped. His father choked on his wine.

Yes, he had.

'Are you saying…?' His mother clasped her hands beneath her chin, eyes glistening.

'I've asked Eve to marry me…' he met Eve's gaze and she held it, for strength, for the confidence to see this through '…and she's said yes.'

George was back to clearing his throat. 'But—I don't understand. You've only known each other a month. How can you know each other enough to—?'

Nate's hand tensed beneath hers as his eyes snapped to his father's. 'I can assure you I know her very well.'

'Is this about the will?' his father said, eyes sharp behind his glasses.

'What are you talking about, George? Our son has just told you he's getting married and you're—'

'I thought you would be happy,' Nate interjected. 'Holt was, after all, one of your dearest clients, closest friends.'

'That doesn't answer my question.'

'I know more about Eve after a month than I knew about you my whole life. Making a home with her will be a joy by comparison.'

His father paled, his mother made the strangest noise, and the very air stilled. The pain in that one statement… He was defending their engagement, he was protecting his mother, and hating his father for daring to expose the truth in front of her.

And Eve couldn't bear it.

'Nate…' his mother started. 'I don't—'

'Leave it, Sue-Ellen. The boy clearly has something to get off his chest, so have at it.'

Nate turned to Eve, his tormented blues making her shiver inside. She squeezed his hand again. 'Why don't I help your mother clear away the dishes, and you two can clear the air?'

'I have a better idea.' Sue-Ellen got to her feet. 'Come with me, Evelyn. I have some champagne I've been saving for such a special occasion. We can enjoy it in the garden room.'

Eve looked to Nate and he gave a slight nod, releasing her hand.

'That's sounds lovely, but a sparkling water will suit me just fine,' she said, following the other woman out and wishing with all her might that Nate was okay. That he *and* his father would be okay.

To say Nate had sat on his resentment for decades, it all came spilling out with surprising ease. Everything he had told Eve, right down to his tattoos and his belief that his father had no pack mentality.

And George took it. Leaning back in his seat, he kept his lips sealed. He didn't interrupt or try to argue back. Just listened.

When finally he was done, his father leaned forward. 'That was quite the list of misdemeanours—'

Nate opened his mouth to object.

'I'm sorry, son, I don't mean that in a derogatory sense, what I mean to say is… Hell…' He raked a weary hand down his face, hazel eyes grave. 'I brought you up like my father did me. And his father before him. We were the breadwinners. We threw ourselves into our work, proved ourselves through it. I didn't question it. I didn't think... I guess I didn't know how to be a different father. I didn't know that's what you needed... I took your rebellion as a sign of your nature, of boredom with this town and its limitations. I saw it as you acting out against it...'

'I *was* acting out, but not because of where we lived. I'd played the moral student, the moral son, got the grades, and you never looked my way for long enough.'

'And you figured bad behaviour would be different?'

Nate swallowed. 'I have regrets, believe me. My intention was always to come back and show you I could have it all—a legal career to be proud of, a wife and a family I actually spend time with. I wanted to show you how it should be done.'

'And you think marrying a Waverly will do that and more?'

'No, Dad. Who her father is doesn't factor into it. I'm marrying Eve because I want to.'

He nodded, the silence stretching between them.

'The thing is, Dad,' Nate said, realising there was more to say, to admit. 'Had I known what you were doing, all those people you were helping, it might have changed things. At least it would have made me see you in a different light.'

'And if you'd told me how you felt long ago, I

would have made strides to be a better father to you, to come home more…'

'I remember Mum asking you to come home, it rarely worked.'

'She did, but then she also knew the good I was doing. And I love that she loved me for that.'

'You'd rather she loved you for the good work you were doing in your absence rather than your presence?' Nate shook his head. 'Dad, really?'

'I know, son, but I'm trying to make up for it now. With your mother. And with you, if it's not too late?'

'Too late?'

'To have that relationship?'

Nate raked a hand through his hair, his father's sincerity choking up his chest.

'So long as we're both living and breathing it's never too late.'

His father smiled, the hint of tears brimming. 'And this marriage, it truly is what you want?'

'More than anything, Dad.'

'How would you feel about an engagement party?'

Ears straining for sounds further inside the house, Eve took a second to register Sue-Ellen's question, then…

'A party?' she blurted.

'Yes, darling. For all George and I have been married for years, we rarely attended functions together. It was partly my fault. I always found it a little nerve-racking being on show like that. Everyone knew him and flocked to his side and I was always a little worried I'd embarrass him.'

Eve recalled Nate saying something similar… Was it possible he'd picked up on his mother's insecurities over the years too?

'Of course, it was all in my head,' she was saying, 'and it's high time I got over it and what better way to do that than to have a wonderful party celebrating your fabulous engagement?'

'What's that I hear?' George's voice was suddenly upon them as both men appeared in the doorway. 'A party?'

Eve shot up, eyes searching Nate's.

How did it go? You okay? Do we need to run, stay…make hay?

She rushed forward, took his hand and he smiled—a *real* all-is-okay smile.

'Don't worry, Evelyn. Me and my boy are fine.' His father hooked his arm around his approaching wife's waist. 'Or we will be. Won't we, son?'

'We will,' Nate confirmed, squeezing Eve's hand.

Sue-Ellen covered her mouth, her eyes welling up. 'And to think, this is what it took…'

'So what was it you were saying about a party?' Nate asked, his voice less certain.

'Your mum suggested we have one to celebrate our engagement.'

'An excellent idea,' George said.

'But I'd rather we didn't have the press getting wind just yet,' Nate said. 'Eve will want to put a statement out at some point and—'

'It's okay, Nate.' She pressed her hand to his chest, sensing he was more concerned about her reaction to it than anything else. And if the party was such a huge step for his mother, it made it all the more important to Eve. 'It makes sense to do something. We have to announce it at some point anyway. We could do something at the station, an intimate gathering of our nearest and dearest. I'm sure Rose would approve.'

'And I would help,' his mother chipped in.

'How about Friday evening?' his dad suggested.

'*Next* Friday?' Eve said.

'You really think you're up to a celebration so soon, Dad?'

'Oh, don't you start, son. It's bad enough with your mother on at me.'

'And your father's been feeling so much better,' the woman herself said.

'Still...' Nate cautioned. 'People will have plans. Friday is only a week away.'

'As soon as people see the invitation from Garrison Downs,' his father said, 'they'll drop everything to be there. You mark my words.'

'They're in full-on muster season, Dad. This is the last thing Rose needs on her plate.'

'If we wait for muster season to be over, it'll be December.'

December. It felt so far away and yet not. She'd be in her second trimester and likely showing.

'Your parents are right, Nate. It makes sense to

have the celebration now. Especially with us wanting to get married so soon.'

Nate looked down at her in his arms. 'Are you sure? Maybe you should speak to Rose first, love?'

Love. She tried to reply and failed, nodding instead.

'That's settled, then,' his father said.

'Oh, how exciting!' His mother's voice cracked, the tears now escaping as she pulled them both into a hug. 'I couldn't be happier for you.'

'I could,' his father murmured. 'I believe a dessert was mentioned?'

'Not for you, there isn't.'

'Come on, Sue-Ellen, a tiny sliver isn't going to hurt.'

She rolled her eyes. 'Caramel slice, anyone?'

It was late when they said their goodbyes, Nate insisting he drive Eve back to the station when his mother offered up his old bedroom. She didn't know whether it was the idea of sharing a room with her that had him rushing her out of the door, or concern for how she felt about it.

But she knew which one she hoped it to be.

The glimpse of old Nate while performing in the presence of his parents had her craving more. Whether it was wise with the way her emotions were spiralling, she didn't care, she just didn't want their loved-up cover to end. So when he saw her into the truck and climbed in beside her, she said, 'Kiss me.'

His head snapped around. 'What?'

'Your mother's looking out the window,' she said, as calm as she could manage, and she wasn't lying. Sue-Ellen was there, keen as any loving mother would be, waving them off.

'She is?'

She nodded and reached into his hair, pulled him close. 'Yes.'

He didn't resist, he didn't initiate it either, and slowly she closed her eyes and kissed him. She kissed him with all the affection she'd been forcing down inside. Telling him with her actions what she couldn't tell him with her words.

He wrapped his arm around her, pulled her in close. So close she swore she could feel his heart beating through his chest, as fast and as unsteady as hers. The cabin became hot, humid, stifling. She wanted to strip him of his clothing, of his blasted mask too. She wanted him as exposed as she felt. As vulnerable, too.

And then he stopped, sucked in a breath as he fell back in his seat. 'Thank God she's already gone.'

She flicked him a look beneath her lashes. 'Sorry.'

'It's okay.' And just like that he was back to cool and composed Nate. His streaked cheeks the only sign of what they'd shared as he started the engine and slammed the truck into reverse. 'If there'd been any doubt in her mind, your kiss would have seen it off.'

'My thoughts exactly.'

Only they weren't. Because her thoughts had been racing with so much more. Her heart was racing with so much more.

You want *so much more if you'd only admit it to yourself.*

She settled back into her seat, left Nate to his thoughts as she lost herself in her own. She didn't intend to fall asleep, but something about her father's truck and having Nate at the helm made her feel cocooned in some way, content almost… the gentle rumble of the dirt beneath the wheels, the deserted moonlit road lulling her into a comfortable slumber. One that she was loath to leave and when the engine cut some time later and Nate reached over to touch her shoulder, she batted his hand away.

'We're home, Eve,' he murmured.

Home? Me and Nate. Home.

She squinted up at the well-lit porch. Rose must have kept the light on for her.

'I'll call you in the morning.'

'You'll…' Her heart plummeted. 'You're not staying?'

'I think I've put Rose out enough already.'

'As if. Without you she never would've kept on top of everything this week.'

'Wait until you tell her you've a party to organise.'

'Your mother and I will take care of that. Rose only has to turn up and look pretty, which she does on a daily basis anyway. No trouble.'

His chuckle was low and slow, his eyes dark as they continued to connect with hers. 'I don't think it's a good idea.'

'What? The party, or you staying?'

He didn't answer.

'Nate?'

He leaned back into his seat, eyed the porch rather than her. 'It makes sense for me to be in Marni tonight. I have a long day of catch-up meetings tomorrow.'

'On a Saturday?'

'A weekend doesn't get in the way of clients that need me. And Dad wants us to go for a drink... I think he's trying to make up for lost time as quickly as possible.'

She straightened against the disappointment that swamped her. 'That's good, Nate. Really good.'

So good it almost took the edge off her disappointment. Almost.

'It's a start.'

'When will I see you again?'

He gave her a surprising smile. 'We have a party on Friday, remember.'

'But that's a week away.'

'Afraid you're going to miss me...?'

Yes, she wanted to scream, *yes*!

Only he was teasing, and she wasn't.

'You wish.' She unclipped her belt and shoved open the truck door, then paused as she caught sight of his motorbike. 'Take the truck though, won't you? It can't be safe on two wheels this time of night.'

He gave her a lopsided grin. 'So you do care...'

More than you know and I want to admit, she thought as she closed the door and headed up the steps to the house.

She didn't look back. Not once. Fear that he would see her for the fraud she was propelling her forth.

Rose was in the hallway with River as she entered, and her sister's tired smile was the last thing Eve needed to see. 'Hey, honey, did you have a nice—? Evie, what's wrong?'

Eve waved her sister down, tried to tell her she was fine and failed at the whole darn lot. Rose opened her arms and pulled her in close and Eve sagged and let it all out. Let Rose hush her and soothe her. See her to bed. She didn't press her for answers, didn't press her for anything.

She was just there, as sisters should be.

CHAPTER TEN

'YOUR FATHER AND I are so proud of you.'

Between tears and smiles, his mother patted his tie into place. A move she had done a hundred times over. He'd thought about stopping her but decided it was far better to let her preen. Especially as he had yet to break the news that they would be moving to London at the end of the year.

'Okay, Sue-Ellen, let the boy go. You'll wear that tie away.'

His father entered the hallway, dressed like Nate in a dark suit, they *looked* like father and son, and Nate felt the fresh bond between them grow. His father kissed his mother's cheek before turning to Nate.

'Can I borrow you a moment?'

'Sure.'

He sent a questioning look his mother's way, but she only shrugged and, pocketing his hands, he followed his father into his study. Watched as he pulled open the drawer behind his desk and took out a small black box.

'I have something for you...or rather, I have something for you to give to Evelyn.'

Nate buried his hands deeper into his pockets. 'You do?'

'It's been in the family for generations, passed down to the eldest son.'

'Another one of those...' Nate tried to tease.

'Another one of those...' his father agreed. 'Though it went to at least one daughter, your grandmother, and since she was still alive when I proposed to your mother, I refused to take it from her. I told her that one day, God willing, I'd have my own child to give it to. And that time has finally come.'

Nate eyed the velvet box in his father's outstretched palm as though it would suddenly grow eight legs and fangs.

'I couldn't help noticing that Evelyn didn't wear a ring and as my mother called this a promise ring it seems perfect, don't you think...? If Evelyn likes it, of course.'

Slowly, Nate took it, opened it up. An oval diamond sparkled back at him, dazzling in its intensity, its meaning too.

'What do you say, son? Will she like it?'

'She'll—' He cleared his throat. 'It's perfect.'

Because it was.

It was Eve in every way. Beautiful. Elegant. Bright.

'And as the woman who's claimed your heart, it's all hers.'

Claimed his heart...

The blood drained from his face. Hot and cold all at once.

'Don't look so worried, son.' His father chuckled. 'The hard part's over already. She's said yes, remember.'

And then he pulled him into a hug, something he hadn't done since Nate was a child.

'I know I haven't told you enough, but I *do* love you, son, and I'm proud of you.'

'I love you too, Dad.' Because he did. It was why it had hurt so much over the years, why it hurt now too.

His mother appeared in the doorway and his father backed up, coughed away the emotion.

'Our car is here,' she said, her own voice laden with emotion.

'Good to go, son?'

Nate nodded and they shared one more look. A look that had Nate wondering, if this was his impassive, workaholic father after all these years, was there a chance that Eve could change too? That one day she'd be ready for such sentiment, such love? Could she trust him with it?

The box pinched into his tightly clenched hand— *don't be a fool.*

Because for all tonight was about their engagement, it wasn't about love.

This was Eve. Eve who refused to love, to trust, to risk it all. Eve who'd run from the very suggestion that it meant more.

Engage head.

Disengage heart.
Simple.
Or so he told himself.

Eve was ready. Physically at least.

Her hair had been styled by Lindy, who it turned out, could turn her hand to anything.

Her make-up was bold and dramatic—red lips, smoky eyes, slight blush—just how she liked it.

Only it felt all wrong.

She felt too made up. Too fake.

'You look beautiful, Bambi.'

She turned to see Rose in the doorway, a glass of bubbles in hand, work gear still on.

'For you…' She lifted the glass and stepped inside. 'It's a non-alcoholic variety, that way no one will be any the wiser when we toast your engagement tonight. Thought you might like to sample it.'

She smiled up at her sister. 'Thanks, Rose.'

'How are you feeling?'

'Nervous.'

That was honest at least.

'Don't be. All will be wonderful, I'm sure.' Rose pressed a kiss to her head. 'Now I need to shower else I'll be greeting our guests in this.'

Eve's smile lifted to one side. 'You still look stunning.'

Rose laughed. 'Now I know you're lying.'

She turned to leave and spied the blue gown Eve had pulled out. About the only thing she'd brought from London that she'd get to wear. Aside from the dress she'd worn to Nate's parents'.

'Is that what you're wearing?'

'Yes.'

Rose turned back to her, the slightest quiver in her lips.

'Rose, what are you…? You're not…'

She wafted a hand at her face. 'I'm sorry, Evie, I just wish they were…'

Her voice trailed off, and Eve knew where she was heading but didn't dare.

'I know,' she whispered.

Rose smiled as she swept from the room, though Eve thought she caught a hiccup-cum-sob, the absence of their parents weighing heavier than ever.

Her gaze drifted to the journal still beside her bed and, without thinking, she crossed the room, picked it up with a trembling hand, willing her mother's presence into being. Her love. Her bond.

Nate had faced his demons and spoken to his father, it was high time she faced hers…

Running her thumb down the gilded gold edge, she let the book fall open. Her mother's handwriting, elegant in its long, looping style, filled the page. Word upon word blurring as tears welled.

The first entry was over twenty-five years old…

I write these words upon instruction from experts who seem to believe it will help. I write these words so that I might find my way back to my daughters, my life, myself. I write these words to commit to my circumstances, and to bend them to suit my needs, the needs of my girls, and the needs of my family. I write these words as I choose to flourish, and no longer to fade.

Eve's breath shuddered through her. 'Oh, Mum.' She wanted to stop but made herself continue. To straighten out her head, she had to straighten out her heart. She knew that now more than ever.

In the pages, her mother's version of events was laid bare. How she'd felt alone, trapped in her own head. She hadn't been able to love Holt. Hadn't been able to love her children. Hadn't been able to love herself. Cold and detached. Disconnected and scared. Until finally she'd been diagnosed. Diagnosed and treated. And when the affair had come to light, her mother's world had crumbled. Their love had been tested and found wanting. It had taken time and understanding on both sides to find their way back to one another. Time in which her father had to move on from Lili and her mother had to forgive. In her beautiful, evocative way, her mother wrote of her hope that one day Holt, too, would forgive himself. For they loved one another and always would. And that was the greatest gift of life—to love and be loved.

Eve sobbed into her fist, clutched the book to her chest. Understanding rocking her to the core. All those years Eve had hated her father, hated the lie she felt they'd *both* portrayed…when it had been no lie at all.

She was the liar. Marrying for all the wrong reasons when, inside, the truth was desperate to break out.

She looked to the window, imagined the spot in the hills where her parents were laid to rest and knew what she had to do—where she had to be.

Throwing on some clothes, she hurried to the stables and mounted Jade. She clicked her into a gallop as soon as she was able and didn't slow until she saw the ancient flame tree. Its branches sprawling out at the peak of Prospect Hill, its orange-red flowers vibrant in the setting sun. Its base littered with wildflowers—yellow, reds, purples, pinks— a cacophony of colour that she'd never paused to appreciate before. The sign of life when life was no more…

She dismounted and took the journal from the saddlebag, led Jade to the tree and the two gravestones resting there. She sank to her knees, her 'Sorry' taken away by the breeze.

She swept her hair out of her face, clutched the journal to her chest. 'I love you and I miss you. And I wish with all my heart that you were both here to guide me now.'

The wind whipped up around her, her hair stinging at her eyes, catching in her mouth.

You know in your heart what's right. Trust it.

Where the words came from, she didn't know… but she was finally ready to listen.

* * *

'Evie, what are you doing?'

Rose accosted her as Eve kicked off her boots, tossing them into the mudroom.

'I had to go and see Mum and Dad.'

'You *did*?' Then she saw the journal in Eve's hand. 'Jeez, you really do pick your moments, sis.'

'I know, I know.' Eve rushed towards the bedroom, Rose hot on her tail. 'But I'm glad I did it.'

'In that case, I'm glad too but your absence has been noted and your future husband isn't looking too happy. I think he's worried you're about to run.'

Eve faltered in her stride.

'I'm not planning on it.' In fact, she was planning on doing the opposite. Whatever the outcome of tonight, she was staying indefinitely. Because the more she thought on it, the more she didn't want to go back to her life in London, not the way it was, and certainly not to the job that hinged on the image of others. Selling falsehoods, bending the truth to suit…

And Garrison Downs finally felt like home again. She wasn't ready to give that up.

She had ideas forming, ideas that involved making the old homestead her home—if they kept the station and her sisters were happy for her to take it on…

'I'll leave you to get ready.'

She nodded and changed quickly, freshening up her make-up, checking her hair. She left the room, following the sound of music and chatter all the way to the ballroom, where she was immediately set upon by every guest. All congratulating her on the news, most genuine, but others…their restraint bordered on hostile. The reason for the latter became apparent when Betty from the pub teetered up to her.

'Don't worry too much, darl, they'll recover.'

'Recover?' Eve said, still getting over the last strained greeting. 'From what?'

'From your Nate being off the market.'

'Oh…*oh*!'

'You really are oblivious, ain't ya, darl? All those loved-up pheromones doing their thing!'

'Uh-huh,' Eve said weakly.

'His return has been the talk of the town, right up there with yours. All the mothers, the fathers too, were hoping their daughter would be the one to snap him up. As for the daughters, well, you can see their tiny broken hearts for yourself.'

She forced a smile. 'Good to know the Marni grapevine is still functioning.'

Betty laughed. 'Always, darl.'

The crowd chose that moment to shift and Nate came into view, his gaze clashing with hers and locking on. Deliciously sexy in a dark suit and skinny tie, hair immaculate, designer stubble too. She felt starved of him, her body aching with it. A week without sight and she wanted to feast on him for evermore.

He leaned to mutter something to his companion, though his gaze didn't leave hers. Then he was striding forwards. Eyes ablaze with what, she didn't know. Eve gulped. The epitome of Bambi caught in the headlights. Unable to move from the danger fast approaching.

He paused a step away. 'Good to see you, Betty.' Though his eyes remained fixed on Eve.

'And you… And I'll just leave you to—' a wave of her finger '—*this.*'

Eve fought the urge to yank her back, wrinkled her nose. 'I'm sorry I'm late.'

His jaw pulsed. 'You're sorry you're late?'

'That's what I said.'

'Not for the riding like a madwoman?'

'You saw that?'

'I saw that.'

Anger reverberated through his words. Anger that she didn't understand.

'You're angry?'

'*Of course I'm angry, Eve,*' he said between his teeth.

She eyed the crowd around them, noticed the discrete looks being cast their way and stepped closer. Lowered her voice. 'I was late. I didn't plan on it. I went to my parents' grave and I lost track of time.'

'You did what?'

'I wanted to make amends. I *did* make amends.'

His eyes flickered, softened, though the tension remained. 'I'm glad you've made your peace with them, but, *Eve*, the way you were riding. I thought we'd gone through this. You can't just do what you want, when you want, how you want. You need to think about the risks. You're a *mother* now.'

His words slammed into her, his accusation too.

'I can ride, Nate. When I was a kid, I could ride better than I could walk.'

'And what if Jade had got spooked? What if she'd thrown you? Then what?'

A memory from her childhood flashed across her mind, a time when a snake had startled her horse and she'd ended up with a broken her arm. She cursed. He was right. How could she be so foolish? What kind of a mother would put her child at risk like that?

But she hadn't been thinking. All she'd wanted was to get back. To him. To this. To find a way through it all that led to happiness, not more pain and regret.

'I'm sorry, I—'

The chime of metal on glass rang through the room, the music stopped and the chatter died away. Eve's heart fading with it.

George Harrington stepped up to the microphone as a glass appeared beside her. Rose. She mustered up a smile, for her sister and the room, and took the drink.

Nate placed his palm against her lower back and the contact pulsed through her. She glanced up at him. Wishing to see the same reaction in him and getting nothing. His smile, his possessive touch, all an act, a performance to project the happy couple. A lie.

His father's toast was a blur, Rose's too. The cheers and the congratulations landing on Eve's deaf ears because all she could hear was Nate's words. *'You can't just do what you want, when you want, how you want... You're a mother now.'*

And what did she know of being a good mother? What did she know of being a good wife too?

She was one of many women in Marni who'd set their sights on Nate, but she was the only one who had done it against her will. And hell, he could do better. He deserved better.

She forced herself to sip at her glass when the room toasted their engagement. Forced herself to smile and play nice when all she wanted to do was run. Run as she had all those years ago.

'I think that makes it my turn to say something…'

Her eyes shot to his, heart in her throat.

Please, no. God, no. No more lies.

'The moment I saw you, Eve, I knew there was something about you…'

He held her gaze as he directed the words at her but spoke to the room. And she was pleading with him. Pleading with him to stop. But his eyes…they were sincere…or was that an act? Was he putting that look there for everyone else but her?

'A connection that caught me in its grasp and wouldn't let me go. Your beauty, your intelligence, your wit, and your fire. Not necessarily in that order…'

The room chuckled and he smiled, taking her

hand in his as he raised it up between them and dug into his pocket with his other.

'I should've done this sooner, but it feels appropriate to do it now in front of our nearest and dearest—'

'Wait, wait!' Rose hurried out. 'I need to video this for Tilly and A— everyone who couldn't make it!'

Ana, she was going to say Ana. Eve gave her sister a smile, her gaze swiftly returning to Nate's pocket, where his hand still rested, and she swallowed the wedge in her throat. Why hadn't she anticipated this? They were engaged. There was bound to be a ring of some sort…

Rose held her phone out. 'Go!'

And Nate chuckled, lowering himself to one knee, all charismatic and perfect, and Eve could almost believe this was real. Not a lie that was eating her up inside.

He pulled the box from his pocket, opened it up. An oval diamond shone out, dazzlingly exquisite but glaring in its meaning. She clutched her throat, eyes watering. Tears, more *blasted* tears.

'Eve, I believe we were destined to meet that night in Marni, our lives taking a simultaneous twist that brought us back to our families at the same time. Our bond was instant and unbreakable.'

The bond was their child. Eve knew it. Nate knew it.

As for destiny, it was right up there with love. The kind of sentiment she would have denied, laughed off even, but not any more. It danced around her heart, teased her, goaded her. Broke her that bit more as more tears came.

'This promise ring has been in my family for generations, an outward sign of that inner bond. Of love and its infinite longevity.'

'But what if it doesn't fit?' she whispered and the people near enough to overhear chuckled. Not realising she meant it in the figurative sense. A ring representing love... Eve and love. She tried to force the two puzzle pieces together, and no side would fit.

Nate took the ring from the box, held her hand in his and said softly, surely, 'We'll make it fit.'

And with that, he slid it over her finger as smooth and as easy as breathing...

Breathing when she wasn't in front of a crowd of people, her emotions rolling wild within her.

'It's perfect,' she choked out and the crowd whooped. Nate swept her up into his arms and she knew what came next, anticipated it even. But nothing could prepare her for the brush of his lips against hers as he stole her breath and her heart in one.

'Thank you,' he murmured, so quiet no one else could hear.

Her lashes fluttered open, gratitude shining down on her.

Gratitude, for what? Continuing the performance? Not running?

The music started up again, the sound jarring her out of her stupor.

'We should dance,' he said.

'Dance?'

It was the last thing she wanted to do. Too jolly. Too free. Too easy. But she let him sweep her onto the dance floor, let him guide their every move. So very aware of every place their bodies touched, so very aware of how fleeting every connection was, as if he couldn't bear it, too.

Remember why you're doing this, Eve.

Remember why he's doing it, too.

For your family. For your child.

And still, she couldn't shift the chill.

While the sham of a marriage ate away at her, the ring on her finger too, she should have been safe in the knowledge that this marriage couldn't hurt her.

But that was before she'd understood her past. Before she'd realised that, for all it could bring pain and hurt, the only bond that truly tied people together for ever was love.

Without it, they had nothing. No joy. No future. No bond.

And she was already hurting. Deeply and unequivocally.

CHAPTER ELEVEN

'GOODNIGHT, SON.'

'Night, Dad. Sleep well.'

Nate closed the door on the guest room his parents were using for the night and made his way back to Eve's.

He'd say he was relieved that the night was over, but his biggest challenge was yet to come.

A night in Eve's bedroom. Alone. Nothing to keep this heat or emotion at bay.

They hadn't slept together since Marni, hadn't even kissed properly…save for the show of carried-away affection outside his parents' house.

Not what he needed to be thinking of right this second.

He tugged his tie undone, unbuttoned his collar. He'd been so angry this evening, angry and fired up on something else entirely.

Stunning in blue satin, she'd taken him over the second she'd appeared. Everything about her accentuated by that dress—her hair, her eyes, her body—but there'd also been a vulnerability about her. A vulnerability that had fed his fears and compounded his alpha instinct—to protect, to possess, to toss her over his shoulder, take her home and never let her out of his sight again.

And it was laughable, not laudable, because she wanted none of that.

And now he had to suppress it all while they slept in the same room together.

What was he? A monk!

Cursing the impossible, he shoved open the door and strode in. There was always the bathtub... 'Eve, I think—'

He froze, his head emptying out as the door clicked shut on its own momentum.

Eve blinked back at him from across the room, just as frozen, just as stunned. 'Did you ever hear of knocking?'

'Did you ever think to shout?'

'Shout what?' She thrust her hands up, a move he *really* didn't need with all that skin on show.

'I don't know! Some warning!'

'Like what?'

'Like, hey, I'm naked!'

And naked she was, unless you counted the scanty piece of blue lace doing a very poor job of concealing anything below the waist.

She folded her arms, which only lured his eyes down. 'You're daring to take issue with my nakedness?'

Her bare breasts shifted with her defiant breath, her small rose-tipped nipples hardening beneath his stare.

'I'm not taking issue with your…'

He cursed. Could the woman not see what she was doing to him?

'You could have fooled me.'

He forced his gaze back to hers—blue eyes blazing, wide and wounded. Her lips, still stained from her lipstick, pouting. Lips he didn't dare get any closer to, and yet he took one step forward.

'I'm not, Eve.'

One brow lifted. 'No?'

Another step. 'I'm taking issue with myself.'

'For what, exactly?'

'For wanting to do this…'

And he quit thinking, quit questioning and tugged her to his chest, claimed her gasp with his kiss and kept on striding until she was up against the wall.

'Tell me to stop and I'll stop,' he rasped out.

'No.' She hooked her leg around his waist, tugged at the lapels of his jacket to drag him closer. 'Don't stop.'

He was in heaven and hell at once. Wanting. Craving. And knowing it was wrong. They needed to talk, they needed to clear the air. 'We should be talking.'

'This first, Nate.'

He cupped her breast, rolled his thumb over its pleading centre, felt it pucker beneath his touch and lowered his head to suck it into his mouth. She cried out, her fingers forking through his hair, gripping him to her. All the while his brain screamed at him to quit. But he was done listening to anything but her.

'I want you,' she whispered, hitching her leg higher, undulating against him. 'I only want you.'

Mouth rough, he grazed kisses back up her body, kissed her deeply as he lifted her legs around him and carried her to the bed. He set her down, shucked his jacket, his tie, his shirt. She rose and stripped his belt, unbuttoned his trousers. Fingers trembling, breath uneven. Desperate. Hungry.

She reached inside his pants, gripped his length and he bucked inside her hold.

'Steady, sweetheart.' He grabbed her wrist, his thighs trembling as he fought the inevitable. 'It's been a while.'

He eased her hand away as he stripped the rest of his clothing and lowered himself to the bed. Encouraging her to lie back as he trailed kisses from her mouth to her breasts, to her stomach, where the wonder of their baby lay…then lower still.

She rocked up as he flicked his tongue over her swollen nub, gripped his head as he circled her, rolling and flicking, letting her every reaction drive his tempo. Letting it feed his own desire too.

'Please, Nate,' she panted, 'I want you.'

He looked up into her eyes, saw the need, the desperation and something else—was it the fear, the vulnerability he'd spied earlier or something else?

He pressed a kiss between her legs and she shifted. 'Please?'

Helpless to deny her, he moved up her body, swallowed her plea with his kiss as he guided her back into the sheets. He searched her lustful gaze as he eased himself inside her. Fighting for control as her heat surrounded him and her eyes seared him, branded him, made him hers. Not that she could know...

She bit her lip, her whimper making him groan. She was taking him to the brink and there was nothing he could do.

The more she moved, the more he moved with her. Faster, harder, deeper.

He was losing it. Every last remnant of control. His body vibrating and tensing in one.

'Eve!' My God, she was beautiful. Stunning. Everything he could ever...

'Nate, I can't... Nate...'

'Let go for me, baby. Let go and I'll catch you.'

I'll always catch you.

His own release came with hers, dizzying and thought-obliterating. His guttural growl so loud he feared there'd be questions from the neighbouring residents come morning.

Morning. He didn't want to think of that now. He didn't want to think of anything but this moment that had felt so perfect in every way.

His body sagged and he rolled onto his back, gazed up at the ceiling. 'That was...'

'Unexpected.' She finished for him.

'I was going to say needed, but unexpected works too.'

She touched her left hand to her stomach, the Harrington ring glinting in the lamplight. An outward sign that she was his, but inside…

Eve would only ever belong to herself.

The chemistry between them didn't change that.

No matter how intense, or perfect, or all-consuming.

It chewed him up inside, a genuine sickness rising that made him want to wretch. He pushed himself to sitting, took a breath so that he could trust his voice. 'I'm going to freshen up.'

He tugged on his pants and headed to the bathroom, felt her confused gaze on him the whole way. He washed his face twice over, brushed his teeth, and still didn't know what to do with himself. The sensation was still there, rolling inside him. He gripped the edge of the sink, stared at the face looking back at him. He'd aged a decade in four weeks, the lines in his brow, the shadows beneath his eyes…

It was getting harder and harder to understand what this was between them. Where the line of convenience ended and it all became real.

'Sorry.'

He spun around. There she was, resting against the door frame. Her hair wild about her shoulders, her eyes soft, smile small. A pale slip thrown over her that ended mid-thigh. And his heart ached for her even as he told it not to.

'What for?'

'For embroiling you in this mess.'

He shook his head, stepped towards her but she moved away. She dropped into the chair before the window, brought her knees to her chest.

The sight tore at his heart. She looked so lost.

'I chose this path, Eve.'

'But you can't want it.'

'The marriage?'

She nodded.

'You're wrong, I want it all. The child. A wife. A family. It's what I've always wanted.'

'I know. You've made that clear from the moment I met you, but you can't want it with me. And you can't want it in London, not when you came back to make a home here.'

'I can and I do. And if we have to do that in London...'

'But your father, your relationship, you're finally getting what you've always wanted.'

'And I can still have that in London. There's video calls, we can visit...'

She was shaking her head, refusing to listen. 'You say that now but...'

'But what?'

'You'll resent me for it eventually.'

'How can you say that?'

'How can you not say that? How can you not see it? You deserve a woman who can love you and give you the life you deserve. Not someone like me.'

'Someone like you?'

'I'm broken, Nate. You know that. I don't know

how to love. I don't know how to trust. I don't know what to trust.'

This woman—so unsure, so lost—was so different from the woman he'd met that first night. She *was* changing, she *was* questioning—was there a chance her heart was shifting with the tide?

'Why don't you start with trusting your heart, Eve?'

She huffed into her knees. 'I did that once and trusted my parents unconditionally. What I saw as their deceit broke me.'

'I thought you'd made peace with the past.'

'I have,' she said quietly. 'But it doesn't change what it did to me. It doesn't change the fact that I don't know how to be a good wife, a good mother...'

'You just have to be you.'

'Are you forgetting the riding incident?'

'No, but you're not either.'

'And what if I'm not enough? If I can't give enough?'

'The fact you're even asking that tells me you will.' He stepped towards her, wanting to pull her into his arms and reassure her. 'You'll be the best mother our child could wish for.'

She looked up at him, searched his gaze. 'I meant for you, Nate. What if I'm not enough for you? My mother and father, they loved one another but she wasn't enough. In her darkest days, she wasn't enough and he went elsewhere and I couldn't bear it if you, if we...'

'Eve!' He dropped to his knees, touched his palm to her cheek. 'I would *never* betray you.'

The very idea had his gut twisted in knots.

'It's easy to say that now when we've not been tested.'

Tested? She was testing him right now!

'I'm not naive, Eve. I know what we're agreeing to.'

'Do you, Nate? Truly? A marriage without love…'

'People marry for a lot less than what we have.'

'Not you.'

'And you never wanted marriage in the first place,' he said, purposely cold, his hand falling to his side. Overly aware that if he said the wrong thing, *did* the wrong thing, it would all be over.

'No, I didn't. But then I didn't want a lot of things that have found me in life.'

She was withdrawing from him, her eyes turning distant.

'What do you want me to say, Eve? How can I make this right?'

'You can be honest with me.'

'I've always been honest with you, and I will *always be* honest with you.'

'Do you love me?'

His chest contracted around his screaming heart, squeezing tight. Her direct question thwarting his every attempt to stay calm. 'How can I say I love you when it's the one emotion you openly run from?'

'That's not an answer.'

'It's a good enough answer for me.'

'I wanted a yes or no.'

'Then no, Eve. I don't love you.'

Because when it came down to it, how could he love a woman who, as soon as her sabbatical ended, would be too wrapped up in work to notice him? How could he love a woman who by her own lips could never love him back?

She stared back at him, so quiet, so calm, the silence deafening as his heart continued to blare. Then she blew out a breath, looked to the dark outdoors and the moonlight dancing in the gum trees.

'And I won't be a hypocrite, Nate.'

'A *what*?'

'I resented my parents for what I saw as the lie they presented to the world, to us… What I saw as their *fake* love. When all the while, it was nothing of the sort.'

'What's that got to do with—?'

Her eyes flashed to his. 'We're doing *exactly* what I accused them of, hated them for. Don't you see? Presenting a fake front, a fake marriage, a fake love, and I won't do it.'

'Even for the sake of our child.'

'I'm *doing this* for the sake of our child. I won't turn our child into me! Have them grow up resenting us for being together for all the wrong reasons, or, worse, perceive us as lying to them. I won't.'

'But it doesn't have to be like that.'

'Doesn't it? What about when the distance between us grows because I can't give you what you need?'

He shook his head, defeat heavy on his shoulders. 'So that's it, it's over and you're going to move back to London and take my child with you?'

'No, I'm done selling images, fake or otherwise. I want to make a home here. A new life for myself and our child, one that keeps you in it, whether we get to keep the station or not.'

'But it's not the same, it could never be the same. You know that.'

'I know our child will be happier knowing their parents are living the lives they chose for themselves.'

He stared at her, unwilling to believe this was happening when not minutes before they'd been as close as two people can be.

At least be happy that she's saying in Australia...
But it wasn't enough. He wanted her.

'One day you'll meet the woman that you were destined to love and you'll thank me for it.'

'Thank *you*?' he choked out.

'A child isn't a reason to marry. And neither is some ancient marriage clause. I release you from your promise, Nate.' She eased the ring from her finger and placed it in his palm. 'Find someone who deserves this, someone who loves you as you do them. Find your happiness.'

'We can be happy together.'

'Without love?' She closed his hand around the ring, pressed a kiss to his forehead and rose up, her eyes so sad they crushed him whole. 'You can't be happy...and I'm not sure I can either.'

She climbed into bed, pulled the blanket over her, and rolled away. The room far too quiet with the roar inside his head, his heart... He opened his hand, looked down at the ring and sagged into the chair.

What did he do? What did he say? His dreams were slipping through his fingers like grains of sand and he couldn't catch them. Because he realised in that moment, with absolute certainty, that he was the only liar in this room.

He loved her and he couldn't tell her.

Damned if he did and damned if he didn't.

And what kind of cruel twist of fate was that?

CHAPTER TWELVE

EVE DIDN'T SLEEP.

She *pretended* to sleep, right up until the point that Nate left the room, and then she packed. Sneaking out at the crack of dawn to hitch a ride on the mail plane before anyone could wake up and confront her.

Despite her desire to be strong and accepting of the future she had now chosen, she wasn't ready to tell anyone that it was over.

It hurt too much. The idea of not marrying Nate, of not being bound together...

So she'd left Rose a note:

Gone to Melbourne to see Ana. I'll call you later.
Eve x

And fled.

Though this was different from all those years ago when she'd run with no intention of returning. This time she was coming back and she would face it all.

But first, she needed to face the last piece of her painful past—Ana.

A meeting that was long overdue and the only thing that she could think to do that would heal rather than hurt. She should've spoken to her half-sister months ago. Done as her sisters had and welcomed her in.

Not pushed her from her mind to tackle what she saw as the more pressing issue of the two—

Issue?

Ana wasn't an issue. She was her sister. Her blood. Another unbreakable bond.

So here she was, standing on the streets of St Kilda, staring at the front of the sweetest little Hungarian restaurant owned by Ana's grandparents. She'd tried her home and a neighbour had told her she'd find Ana and her 'lovely family' here.

She'd smiled her thanks, asked for directions, and hurried away before a tear could escape. *Lovely family.* Rose and Tilly had been lovely too. But Eve?

Heaven knew how Ana saw her and she only had herself to blame.

She stepped towards the door and paused. The scent of food had her taste buds tingling, and she could hear the muffled sound of voices and laughter, but the restaurant was closed. They must be preparing for service.

She peered through the glass. Wooden floors, bentwood chairs, crystal chandeliers and prints of an ancient city filled the walls. An eclectic delight—warm and inviting—but what really caught Eve's attention were the four people sitting around a table in the middle of the room. Four people with love in their eyes and cheer in their voices. Ana and her family.

Eve smiled, the sight warming her even as it labelled her the outsider once more.

At that moment Ana turned, her eyes narrowing and widening just as quick as her chair scraped back and Eve jerked away. She'd intruded on their moment. She should've knocked, should've messaged, should've…

The door swung open. 'Eve!'

She lifted a weak hand. 'Hi, Ana.'

'What are you—why are you—?' Ana shook her head as her mother came up behind her. Same dark hair, same slight frame, though her eyes were a rich brown. Kind, too.

'Ana, who is it?'

'Mum, it's—this is Eve. Holt's daughter.'

Now they were both staring at her and she knew she needed to speak up, say something before they thought she was as deranged as she felt. There was so much she wanted to say and she was struggling to latch onto any one thing. The past, the present, the future that was so uncertain. But nothing would come except tears. They streamed down her face and Ana leapt forward, pulling her into her chest.

'It's okay, Eve,' she soothed. 'It'll be okay.'

Eve shook her head, wanted to apologise, instead she let them usher her inside. Ana's mother and grandparents set about bringing her food, water, and some drink they said was good for the nerves. Though Eve couldn't really taste it. All she was aware of was the love in the room. The love and the care. And she felt relieved.

Relieved to know that all those years where their father had kept Ana out of their lives, her life had been no less rich, because she'd had this.

'I'm sorry, Ana,' she managed at last. 'I should've come sooner.'

Ana gave her a shy smile. 'I'm just relieved that you're here now…and if it's not too bad to say, I'm also a little relieved that you can cry. I had my doubts.'

Eve winced and Ana gave her a nudge. 'I am kidding…well, maybe just a little.'

She gave a choked laugh and Ana wrapped her into another hug. 'So do you want to tell me why you're here when you've only just got engaged to that sexy hunk of a lawyer?'

And just like that Eve was crying again. Uncaring that she had an audience of four. Six if you counted the two chefs prepping in the open kitchen behind, their curious gazes suggesting they heard more than they ought.

But what did it matter anyway? The story of her failed engagement would hit the press at some stage so she might as well get used to it.

'Rose! Rose!'

Nate chased the woman across the yard, gave no thought to the fact he was wearing the same clothes from the night before. His only thought was Eve and the fact she had disappeared into thin air.

He'd spent the night in her father's study, seeking a way to release the sisters from the marriage clause. Ploughing his fitful energy into something that could help rather than hinder the woman that he loved.

Rose stopped, her shoulders sagging, her head dropping forward.

'Rose?'

He came up behind her and she turned to face him. 'What is it?'

His nerves pricked at her tone, the look in her eye…

'Where is she?'

'So, you care where she is, but you don't care enough to love her?'

His frown was sharp, the spear through his heart sharper still. 'What?'

'I rang her this morning, after I found her note.'

'Her note? What note?'

'Telling me where she'd gone. I rang her and she told me how you couldn't love her.'

'That's not—it's not—' God, it sounded so awful, so cold and callous. 'I had no choice, Rose. You know Eve. You know what she's like. I feared she'd run.'

'And in your fear, you what? *Lied* to her?'

'I was lying to myself, too. Please, Rose. I've spent the night trying to find a way out of this marriage clause. Determined to give her something, a thread of hope, anything! I didn't mean to fall asleep. I didn't mean to let her slip away. I can't…'

He thrust both hands into his hair. 'Please, Rose, I need to get to her. I need to make this right.'

'You mean tell her the truth?'

'Yes!'

'Because you do love her, don't you?'

'Yes! With all my heart, I love her. And I know she doesn't want to hear it, but I can't go another day without her knowing it.'

Like the sun coming out from behind a cloud, Rose grinned. 'In that case I'll do more than tell you, I'll fly you. To Adelaide at least, then you're on your own.'

'Why? Where is she?'

'Melbourne. Visiting Ana.'

His heart eased just a little. She was continuing her journey, making amends with her family... He was glad of it. Even if he'd rather have her in his arms right now.

'Are you coming?' Rose said, when he didn't move.

'Absolutely!' He fell into step beside her.

'But, Nate...' She paused, tilting her Akubra up so that she could pin him with her eyes. 'Break her heart again and I'll break you, is that clear?'

'Break her heart...?'

How could he break her heart if she refused to give it to him...?

'I mean it, Harrington.'

So did he...

'I'd rather die than hurt her again.'

* * *

Eve was so full.

Emotionally and physically.

Ana's grandparents, Dori and Zoltan, were firm believers that a full stomach made for a happy heart, and she did her best to oblige. Though she knew, without Nate, her heart would never be so again.

'Now, you should try our apple strudel, it's delicious,' Dori was saying, her wise old eyes bright and encouraging.

'I don't think I could eat another bite.'

'I think we've fed her enough,' said Lili, coming to her rescue. The other woman's continued kindness moving Eve to tears when she thought of how she'd once hated the faceless woman. Dad's mistress.

But reading Mum's journal, then hearing it from Lili herself. The way she had genuinely loved her father. How their relationship had been born of circumstance and misunderstanding. A belief that his marriage had been over and there had been nothing left to ruin, nothing left to save either.

How wrong they had all been.

But the biggest thing was Lili's lack of regret. Because meeting Holt had given her Ana and she wouldn't change that for all the world.

'Thank you,' Eve blurted. 'All of you. For taking me in, for letting me talk and explain and fix things.'

Lili took her hand and gave it a squeeze.

'We're family,' Ana said, scooting into her side.

'Family always has time to listen and be there for one another. And I'm so happy to have sisters. *Three* sisters!'

Eve touched her head to Ana's. 'Me too.'

'Who on earth…?' Dori frowned at the window. 'Zoltan, there's a man peering through the glass. Go tell him we're not open for another hour.'

Zoltan stood up with a grumble. 'I don't know why we bother putting signs up in the window when people just—'

'Wait!' Ana's head lifted. 'Eve, isn't that—?'

'Nate!' Eve shot to her feet, her heart soaring with her, scarce able to believe it was him, but her heart would know those eyes, that hair, that mouth anywhere. He looked harrowed, desperate…was it all for her?

He's here, isn't he? Tracking you down?

'As in Nate the lawyer you were engaged to?' Lili asked, but Eve was already moving, numb to anything but him.

'Yes, Mum,' Ana said for her. 'And I think we should give them some privacy.'

Chairs scraped back as Eve pulled open the door.

'Eve!' He launched forward, his tortured gaze lighting a fire beneath her feet that had her backing up.

'Nate?' So soft, so confused. 'What are you doing here?'

'I had to see you.' He hesitated. 'But I can leave and talk to you later. Once you've done what you came to. I don't want to intrude. I just—I had to see you.'

Eve looked to the back, to the swinging door that marked the mass exodus of Ana and her family. Though she had the oddest sense that there were four sets of ears straining to listen on the other side.

'If you're worried about me, you needn't be,' she said, eyes coming back to him, shoulders righting as she found strength in the presence of her extended family. 'I'm grateful that you told me the truth and—'

'That's just it, Eve, I didn't tell you the truth and it's been killing me ever since. Even more because I know you struggle to trust, but I was lying to myself too. I was scared. So scared you were going to run, and I was this close to having everything. You, the baby, a family of my own. I couldn't risk it.'

'Risk what, Nate? I don't understand.'

He closed the gap between them, his hands gentle on her cheeks as he tilted her face to his. 'Then let me be clear. No lie. No twisting of the truth to suit some ancient clause, or duty to our baby... I love you, Eve. I loved you the moment we met and I will continue loving you whether you want me to or not. Because love isn't something that we get to choose or get to control, it just is.'

Her lips parted as her breath left her. Both head and heart struggling to catch up with all he had said, to *believe* all he had said.

'It just is?' she repeated dumbly.

'I'm sure there's a better way to put it, but right now...'

She shook her head to try and clear it. He loved her. He truly loved her.

'You can refute it all you like, Eve! Refuse it, reject it, all the r's, but it doesn't change the fact that I love you!'

She covered his hands on her cheeks, found her voice. 'Can I *return* it?'

His brow furrowed, his hands slipping away. 'As you would an item from a store...?'

'No, silly...' She choked on a laugh—disbelief, happiness, love filling her chest to the brim. She looped her arms around his neck, breathed in his glorious scent. 'Maybe I should have used the word reciprocate, that's an "r".'

'Reciprocate?' he rasped, eyes widening. 'You mean...'

She nodded and smiled and cried. 'I mean, I love you, Nate. I think my heart has known for a while but my head took a while to catch up.'

'Why didn't you tell me?'

'Because I was confused and I was scared. Scared of trusting my heart and having you break it. Scared I wouldn't be enough for you and I would trap you into a marriage that you'd one day regret and resent me for.'

'Never, Eve. I swear it.'

She smiled softly. 'I'll remind you of this conversation again in ten years' time...'

His mouth twitched and she leaned that bit closer, wanting so much to kiss him. 'You can remind me of it every decade here on in and I'll tell you the same.'

She toyed with the hair at his nape. 'Is that so?'

'Yes.' He hooked his hands around the base of her spine. 'But what about you? Will you regret it, resent me for it?'

'Never, Nate.' She pressed her body into his, purposely using his words. 'I swear it.'

'In which case, Evelyn Waverly, would you do me the honour of becoming my wife?'

He'd used her full name intentionally, she knew it, bringing something of her father into the moment, and her heart bloomed—no regret, no pain. 'Yes, I'll marry you.'

And then she kissed him, long and deep, right up until the point that the rear door swung open, and Ana and her family fell through it.

'I'm so sorry, Eve!' Ana exclaimed. 'Nagypapa, I told you not to lean on the handle!'

Nagypapa blushed and Eve laughed. Her adoration swelling for them all. She glanced up at Nate, who was blushing almost as much as the rest of them.

'Everyone, this is Nate. Nate, this is Ana and her wonderful family.'

'Hi, everyone,' he said as Ana came forward and did the introductions properly, keeping Eve tucked into his side as if he'd never let her go again.

And that suited her just fine. She was exactly where she belonged.

She touched a hand to her stomach…

We both are.

EPILOGUE

Garrison Downs,
South Australian Outback,
late November

'EVIE, ARE YOU ever coming out of there?' Rose called through the dressing room door. 'Nate's going to think you've fled on the mail plane again if we don't hit the aisle soon.'

'I'm coming! I'm coming!' Eve looked over her shoulder at Lindy, who was still fussing over some detail at the rear. 'Am I ready?'

Lindy backed away and gave a nod. 'You *look* ready, but only you can decide if you're truly ready. Marriage is a huge step.'

Not the effusive answer Eve wanted to hear, but then Lindy was right. This was a huge step. Massive!

And it wasn't helping her nerves…or her jelly-like legs. If she wasn't careful, Bambi was going to make a return and that was the last thing she needed.

Taking a breath, she tugged open the door. 'Rose,

you're going to have to hold onto me tight because these legs aren't feeling so hot right now and—what's wrong?'

Her sister was doing a fine rendition of Munch's, The Scream.

'*Rose?*'

She gave the smallest shake of her head, her glossy brown hair quivering with the move.

'Oh, no, what is it? What have I done?'

Eve teetered up to the full-length mirror and froze, finding herself doing the exact same. Munch would be proud.

'I look like…'

'Mum,' Rose said, joining her before the mirror, the satin of her blush pantsuit barely rustling.

It had been Rose's idea for her to wear their mum's wedding dress. They were similar in so many ways—tall, slim, blonde, blue-eyed. But it was more than that, it was a sense of feeling. A bond. A bond Eve had so desperately wanted to regain and she finally felt as though she had.

'It's perfect on you.'

The strapless mermaid dress had been inspired by Mum's love of Old Hollywood, the ivory satin handstitched by her favourite designer in Paris, too. With the pointed sweetheart neckline, ruched bodice, and flowing skirt, it was everything her mum had been—cultured, elegant and beautiful beyond words.

And now Eve was wearing it.

'She'd be so proud.' Rose swept a loose curl over Eve's shoulder. '*I'm* so proud.'

Her voice cracked and Eve balked. 'Don't be starting with the waterworks, Rose! You'll—'

'Is she ready yet?' Tilly burst into the room, surprisingly swift considering the floor-length satin blue dress she wore. Her gaze lighted on Eve and she came to an abrupt halt, rocking on her heels as Ana followed suit, her dress identical in style to Tilly's but mint green.

Now they were both staring at her, tears welling. 'Not you guys as well!'

'I'm sorry, I can't help it.' Tilly flapped a hand over her face. 'Seeing you in Mum's dress... I always thought you looked like her but this...this is so poignant and I'm... I'm...'

Ana stepped forward, taking Tilly's hand in hers. 'You do look beautiful, Eve.'

And they looked like sisters. Ana's brown hair flowing as free as Tilly's blonde waves, their obvious love as uniting as their Waverly blue eyes.

'I want to hug you!' Tilly said. 'But I'm scared I'll crease you!'

'I can take some creasing.' Eve held out her arms. 'Especially if it'll stop you all crying.'

They hugged and, darn it, Eve felt a tear escape. 'My make-up is never going to survive the day.'

'Something tells me your groom won't care,' Ana said as they all broke apart. 'Not if that display in Nagymama and Nagypapa's restaurant was anything to go by.'

'Ooh, do tell us more,' Tilly said and Eve blushed.

'Let's *not* do that.'

Rose laughed. 'Oh, we're definitely doing that, but later. First we need to get you married.'

'And before we do that, I have something for you!' Tilly reached into the front of her gown and pulled out a blue pocket square. 'It was Dad's…' Tears fresh in her eyes, she handed it to Eve. 'I figured it could be your something blue.'

'Oh, Tilly!' Eve fed it through her shaky fingers, raised it to her lips and closed her eyes. 'Now I have them both with me…'

'You have us all,' Tilly said, wrapping her arm around Ana to make sure she knew they included her too. 'Now you have your something blue from Dad, your something old from Mum—what's your something new?'

'My—my underwear…?'

They all laughed, and Ana offered out her hand. In it was a small velvet pouch with the logo of Ana's handmade jewellery store. Something Eve had learned all about after her and Nate's extreme PDA in Melbourne.

'I was going to save this as a leaving gift for your honeymoon, but…'

Eve took it from her, marvelling at her sister's generosity, her talent too.

'You already made our wedding rings, Ana, you really shouldn't have—*oh, my*!' In her palm fell a silver chain with a white diamond-embellished swan. 'It's— It's…'

'It was something Nate said to me when he came to Melbs and I thought—well, I hope you like it.'

'Like it? I *love* it!' She tugged her sister in for a hug. 'And I love you!'

'I love you, too.'

'And I love you all, but we really need to get moving.' Rose took the necklace from Eve and looped it around her neck.

'Best stick that hanky where I had it, sis,' Tilly said. 'You're gonna need it.'

Eve eyed the front of her gown and shrugged— if it was good enough for Princess Tilly...

'And don't forget your flowers,' Rose instructed.

Plucking their rose bouquets off the bed, Eve's the largest of them all, they left the room. Ana and Tilly first, then Eve and Rose. All quiet with their thoughts.

It wasn't far to the ballroom, but it felt like an eternity as Eve took in the hallway and the memories of old, a smile touching her lips as she focused on the good. The echoes of happy chatter, her mother tinkling on the piano, her father's deep and rumbling laugh...

Family. Memories. Love. And hope. She'd let them all in and she'd found happiness.

The only person not here to witness it was Granny, but Eve and Nate would see her very soon. The first stop on their honeymoon across Europe was London. And they'd fill her in on every glorious detail...

'Here we go, sis,' Rose murmured as they reached the entrance to the ballroom.

The double doors swung open as if by magic, and though the grand room with its ivory panelled walls, subtle gilt detailing and twin chandeliers was decorated as she'd planned, it still took her breath away. Blush and cream flowers adorned every surface, every chair, every set of French doors that showcased a glorious end to spring outdoors.

The music changed tempo, the officiant signalled the room and row upon row of guests stood and turned, but all Eve saw was Nate. Waiting for her.

He looked over his shoulder and caught her eye, his mouth lifting to the side—a look she had come to know well. He liked what he saw. And so did she.

I love you, she mouthed.

I love you, too.

And then Tilly and Ana stepped between them…

'Patience, Bambi.' Rose eased her back as she tried to follow. Too eager. Too quick. 'You know you get to spend the rest of your life with him, right?'

'I know. I just can't wait.'

And she couldn't.

I get it, Mum, she mentally whispered. *Love and all its many peculiar facets. I finally get it.*

* * * * *

*Look out for the next story in the
One Year to Wed quartet*
Cinderella and the Tycoon Next Door
by Kandy Shepherd

*And if you enjoyed this story,
check out these other great reads from
Rachael Stewart*

My Unexpected Christmas Wedding
Off-Limits Fling with the Heiress
Consequence of Their Forbidden Night

All available now!

HARLEQUIN
Reader Service

Enjoyed your book?

Try the perfect subscription for Romance readers and get more great books like this delivered right to your door.

See why over 10+ million readers have tried Harlequin Reader Service.

Start with a Free Welcome Collection with free books and a gift—valued over $20.

Choose any series in print or ebook. See website for details and order today:

TryReaderService.com/subscriptions